T0101979

ADVANCE PRAISE FOR *CARTOONS*

Hilarious and extravagant, Kit Schluter's *Cartoons* had me laughing out loud within moments. A fantastical collection.

—**RIKKI DUCORNET**, author of *The Plotinus*

The true surrealist is unblinking, convulsive, and cheerfully open to the mysterious flow, into their texts, of mythic and archetypal elements operating beyond their conscious control. In *Cartoons*, Kit Schluter vaults into the zone of Julio Cortázar, Richard Brautigan, and late Giorgio de Chirico, where the reader breathes the air of pure freedom attained rattling inside the chains of self.

—**JONATHAN LETHEM**, author of *Brooklyn Crime Novel*

Kit Schluter's translations have already established him as a major intellect . . . His fictions, which are unlike anything by another living American writer, are sure to establish him as a unique and exciting new talent, for fans of Japanese folktales, Max Porter, Marcel Schwob, and *The Simpsons*.

—**CATHERINE LACEY**, author of *Biography of X: A Novel*

One of the best story collections of this young century.

—**SEBASTIAN CASTILLO**, author of *SALMON*

As if the world were a great Glass Snowball, Billy the Kit transforms reality with a single flick of the wrist. With a simple Shake, he brings objects to life and calls up voices from the void, chronicling their impossible adventures that lead us to the absurdity we'll have to confront if we want to be able to stomach our lives.

—**MARIO BELLATIN**, author of *Beauty Salon*

Kit Schluter's *Cartoons* broadcast body horror with the precociousness of a child. It's like he recruited Aesop, Glen Baxter, David Cronenberg, and Tintin to guest star on *The Simpsons*. Whether through fable or illustration, archetypes are shaped from our collective dreamlife and waking mundanity into a hateful microwave, lovesick parrot, girl of paper, numerous sentient household objects, even the perfect translator, the latter of which suggests this book has more to confess about its author than you'd guess. We wake and grow up watching *Cartoons*.

—**EVAN KENNEDY**, author of *Metamorphoses*

Cartoons is just so charming; it's somehow already a classic. Like Wycliffe's Bible, which gave us the words "crime" and "frying pan" and "birthday," here is a language clear and fresh enough to give a fairy tale the eerie force of law. Like Shklovsky's *Zoo, or Letters Not About Love*, these erudite and lucid reveries weave zigzag webs of silly string around a wound we don't quite dare look in the eye. Kit Schluter is the sort of magician who makes children go very still. We're too busy having our belly buttons tickled to notice he's touching our heart.

—**YASMINE SEALE**, poet and translator of *The Thousand and One Nights*

Cartoons is hardly a literary work—as Kit Schluter himself notes in his preface—and yet it's also supremely literary, as if "literature" here were more of a unique power than a mode of writing: the power to do whatever you want—whatever you truly require—free of shame. And the result is liberatory and riveting.

—**PABLO KATCHADJIAN**, author of *Thanks*

CARTOONS

KIT SCHLUTER

Cartoons

CITY LIGHTS BOOKS

SAN FRANCISCO

Copyright © 2024 by Kit Schluter
All Rights Reserved.

Cover and text design by Kit Schluter

Library of Congress Cataloging-in-Publication Data

Names: Schluter, Kit, author, illustrator.
Title: Cartoons / Kit Schluter.
Description: San Francisco, CA : City Lights Books, 2024.
Identifiers: LCCN 2023054629 (print) | LCCN 2023054630
    (ebook) | ISBN 9780872869288 (paperback) | ISBN
    9780872869066 (epub)
Subjects: LCGFT: Experimental fiction. | Short stories. | Essays.
Classification: LCC PS3619.C4356 C37 2024 (print) | LCC
    PS3619.C4356 (ebook) | DDC 818/.609—dc23/eng/20231128
LC record available at https://lccn.loc.gov/2023054629
LC ebook record available at https://lccn.loc.gov/2023054630

City Lights Books are published at the City Lights Bookstore
261 Columbus Avenue, San Francisco, CA 94133
citylights.com

CONTENTS

TABLE OF ILLUSTRATIONS

*. . . the story is entirely true,
since I imagined it from end to end . . .*

BORIS VIAN

PREFACE

Late one night in early 2017, I was walking along Isabel La Católica, the street on which I lived when I first arrived in the city I now call home. I must have been particularly lost in thought because I jolted to attention, finding myself about to plant my right foot directly into the middle of a gaping hole where a sewer cap should have been. Stumbling to the side, I averted disaster...

Or so I thought, because when I righted myself, I saw, in the dim orange light of the street lamp, that this was unlike any sewer hole that I had ever encountered before. Hundreds upon hundreds of cockroaches were crawling in and out of it—in and out, *in and out again* in a seemingly liquid swarm. And off to the side, a group of them was consuming the body of their dead companion (had they killed him? was I next?), while still more were scuttling off to other unknown terminals of the night (the shadows of my very own kitchen, I was sure of it).

Of course, I felt scared . . . and disgusted. But alongside my fright there was also a voice, a voice instructing me that if I did not learn quickly—and by *quickly* the voice meant *instantly*—to love the cockroach, I risked losing my mind. So, right then and there, I decided that, yes, I did love the cockroach. Yes, it went without saying: I had always loved the cockroach . . .

And as a fresh blast of sunlight instantly changes the mood of a cloudy day, so my change of heart altered the scene before me, which had just paralyzed me with disgust, into one of the most resplendent examples of Nature's abundance that I had ever glimpsed. I loved the cockroaches' liquid manner of striding in unison, their cannibalistic mourning ceremony! This was the pure will to live on display before me. I admit that, in its indestructibility, I sensed the cockroach's superiority to the human; in its lack of sentimentality, its superiority to even myself.

Now, many of the pieces in this book—which I began after, yet still in the vicinity of, this encounter—were written in a similar way. Concerned more with personal psychological experiment than anything literary at first, I found myself writing until I stumbled upon an overwhelming concern, an unresolved curiosity, a sense of repulsion, some particularly charged node of sentiment, and instead of letting it get the best of me, chose to open my attention to its particularities. I found I could disarm a feeling if I only picked its dynamics apart into characters and let them, as they say, have at it amongst themselves.

What resulted were playful scenes which staged my own questions at a remove, allowing me—now us—to watch them as a spectator. I've taken a liking to calling them my little 'cartoons.'

30TH BIRTHDAY STORY

It was my thirtieth birthday and, for all intents and purposes, things were going well. I was relatively content with my life, loved my friends, and felt ready to shed the various skins I'd worn throughout my twenties. To celebrate, I treated myself to a big lunch at home, letting myself eat all the foods I like so much, but which, given a certain autoimmune condition I have, provoke serious problems if I eat them too often: candies and donuts and other bready, sugary delights; a big, fat cheeseburger. "Everything in excess can kill you," my mom's old boyfriend told me when I was in high school. "... Even cheeseburgers."

It was my dog Xochi's birthday, too. Who knows when she was actually born (we found each other on the street), but I had decided for festivity's sake to share the date with her. So I bought a steak and cooked it up with lots of salt. I cut it up into little bits and, with my housemates, fed them to her, repeating phrases of encouragement like, "Feliz cumpleaños,

3

Xochi," and, "Muy bien, Xochi...*muy* bien." Afterwards, she licked my pant leg happily, and expected more steak.

Xochi's first year in the house had been, to put it optimistically, full of learning experiences for the both of us. Under her unceasing cloud of mayhem I had suffered the casualties of a laptop (only a year and a half old), my cowboy boots (one of the toes of which she chewed clean through, one of which simply disappeared), my favorite jacket (which she had opened a particular drawer to locate and destroy), and a first edition of Anne Kawala's *Screwball*, a book I had translated into English, inscribed with a two-page letter to me from Anne herself, which she wrote while visiting my apartment in Mexico City. I'd have to write a whole book, just to convey to you the wreckage.

But these losses aside, I had to admit that Xochi had been a positive addition to my life, a grounding and constant force of mutual love and attention in my home. And there we were, celebrating our birthdays together on the couch. I felt the happiness of a thirty-year-old, and she felt the happiness of a one-year-old. I could hear it in her snores.

Around three in the afternoon, I got a knock at the door. This seemed strange to me, because I wasn't expecting anyone. Moreover, I'd told my friends that I wanted to spend the afternoon alone, as a gift to myself, and had gone so far as to tape up a NO VISITORS sign on my front door. Even so, the knock came again, a bit more insistent this time. Xochi woke up and waddled to the door, clumsily whiffing at the air. Putting down my notebook, I walked over too, feeling interrupted, and opened up.

What I saw was peculiar, though I can't say I was entirely surprised. Before me stood three of myselves, although none was exactly me. There was myself at twenty, all mopey and poetic, and alongside him, introverted and overexcited, myself at ten. Then, in a little wheeled incubator which the child was diligently pushing along, equipped with tubes and the rhythmic beeping of his tiny heartbeat, there was myself at precisely zero, a little blueberry-eyed fetus on life support, looking ready to be delivered into the world. I didn't know what to say, but before I had time to decide on a strategy, I found myself, out of habit, inviting them in.

Their entrance was awkward. As were my efforts at hosting. We all had trouble making sense of how to move together through my narrow kitchen while introducing ourselves and exchanging niceties. The ten-year-old tripped on the raised lip of the living room's threshold, causing the baby in that scientific contraption to plop over onto his face and scream into the fabric, all tangled up in wires and tubes. The beeping was getting faster, and no one knew what to do (the three clarified that they, themselves, were hardly acquainted), until we decided to just kind of . . . jiggle the cart until the fetus had flipped over again onto his back and his heartbeat had resumed its normal speed. Finally, after another minute or so of cordialities and nervous laughter, I asked them why they had come. In the meantime, I had actually grown quite curious.

Call me ageist, but I had assumed that the one of myselves who was going to do the talking was the twenty-year-old. But the one who opened his mouth first was the ten-year-old. He used the word "random" a lot, and many other words he claimed to have made up, such as "noodlebunker," which apparently referred to a sort of winged dragon he had invented, and other terms I felt I'd known at some point but had since forgotten. His sentences often exploited alliteration, which he emphasized by raising his voice at each repeated consonant.

"K-it . . . We've C-ome C-alling be-C-ause, C-uriously, you C-ouldn't possibly C-onceive the C-onse-Q-uences of your a-C-tions."

"E-X-C-use me?" I asked, mocking his S-tupid way of S-peaking.

"Don't mo-CK young CH-ristopher," added the twenty-year-old with a win-K.

"Ye-S, your S-i-X-ty-year-old S-elf S-ent u-S to S-ay S-omething S-eriou-S. He S-aid you S-imply mu-S-t know . . ."

"Okay, umm," I said. "I'm ready when you are."

"TH-ere are TH-ree TH-ings he TH-ought—"

"Oh, sweet infant!" cried the twenty-year-old, whose way of speaking was as sad, maudlin, and falsely poetic as

6

the ten-year-old's was cloying and insufferable. "While you orate so, our honeyed hours do while away! Until the end of our lofty, B-razen existences that B-oy would B-reathe such B-reathless, like-consonanced phrases, never arriving at the slaking of any curiosity whatsoever. So, prithee . . . onto my own back allow me to hoist such responsibility! But first: assure my fruitlike heart that you, your fruitlike self, shall ripen with the burden of what I am to tell you."

"Yeah, yeah," I said. "That seems fine."

"*Seems?* I know not seems! A firmer agreement. A hand-shake—firm, I say, as John Clare would have had it."

I sighed and extended my arm, already tired of this clown show, and shook hands with my twenty-year-old self. He motioned toward the ten-year-old, whose hand I also shook. (A strong handshake for such a saccharine kid.) Then he motioned toward the fetus, as well.

"What? I have to shake the fetus's hand, too?" I asked.

The twenty-year-old me nodded gravely, and Xochi stirred from sleep.

"But he's completely sealed away in there!"

This time he shrugged, and motioned again. Xochi cocked her head as I walked over to the medical case.

I started kind of . . . stroking (how else to say it?) stroking his container uncomfortably, and looked down at the face I had thirty years ago to the day, soft and red in its lack of experience. Xochi started growling. And I looked at the

7

twenty-year-old to see if he had accepted my gesture. He nodded in approval, and I sat back down.

"Are we ready?" I asked.

"Yes! Now! The *première chose* of which we've been informed—"

At first it was just a confused yipping, but Xochi's exclamations quickly twisted into an uncontrollable howl. She had never much known how to deal with company at home, especially that of strangers, and, as her excitement built, her need for physical expression exceeded that body of hers with its little coordination. She flopped over on her back and began heaving loud breaths, the air catching in her throat. The ten-year-old started to laugh at her. Then Xochi began to buck, sprinting in insane circles around my living room, colliding with glasses and bottles, tubes of paint and books, throwing my papers to the floor. And before we could stop her, she had knocked the fetus's container to the ground and begun chewing on its wires. One wire snapped between her teeth and, in the moments I spent before fading entirely out of consciousness, I heard the beeping of the fetus's heartbeat become a constant drone, and I saw the twenty-year-old version of myself poof into a cloud of dust and blow away, and I watched the ten-year-old wither too, repeating the sounds of the letter *K*, and I watched the fetus grow up and up and up—while I felt my own self crumpling, as if the breath were being vacuumed from my lungs—

aging until he had come to replace myself at thirty: a naked, hairy adult body stuffed into that medical apparatus meant for bodies delivered too soon, my nose and cheeks and lips hardly recognizable as they squished up against the glass, like a little kid making funny faces.

CIVIL DISCOURSE

This morning I had to punish my dog for the mess she made while I was sleeping.

Pulling her by the scruff of the neck toward all the things she'd destroyed, I asked, "Do you eat my books and break my dishes and piss in my shoes all because you can't talk?"

"I watch you ruin everything around you too, and you *can* talk," she answered, but I didn't understand.

"Tell me!" I shouted.

"When you can't talk," she said, "you're not expected to know how to make yourself understood. Shouldn't it be easy to see that's not the case?"

But I didn't understand, and so, I continued shouting.

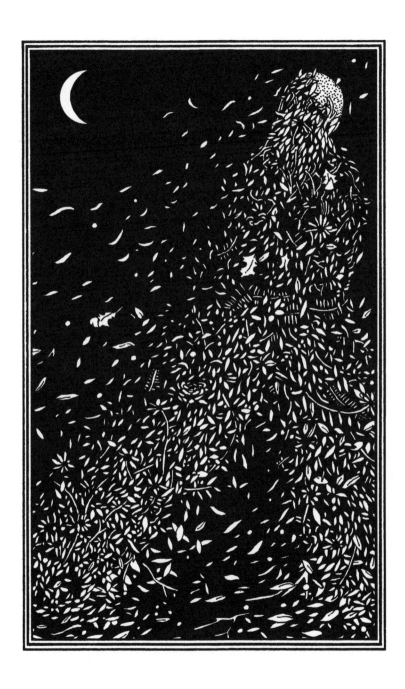

AH, THE BUSHES...!

Down in the city garden, there once lived a man whose palms sprouted unsightly protrusions whenever they got wet. And because they were made of his pale skin, these protrusions resembled little heads of cauliflower. For as long as they lasted, they caused this man intense discomfort, but as soon as they dried, they withdrew entirely into his palms, leaving no trace of prior deformation.

One day the man went to visit an old doctor, who told him — intoning rather grimly — that with each appearance these growths would not only augment in size, but leave increasingly significant traces on his mitts until they sprouted to the size of full-grown bushes. At which point, he continued, almost in a whisper, they would remain forever, weighty and bulbous, even once his hands had dried. From that day on, this man became so afraid of water that he swore he would never so much as bathe again, not even in the stillest waters of the most tranquil streams.

Now, our story picks up at a time by which this man hadn't bathed in well more than a decade, and his body was protected by a thick layer of earth. Whenever it rained, the surface of this earth was watered, and all the little seeds that had blown onto it during recent times would blossom, shrouding him entirely with ferns and moss and the little sprouts that died and flitted away once he had bathed in the sun.

In the early summer month of June, an unusually stormy weather pattern blew in over the city, bringing with it a rain that lasted for so long that not even the dirt encasing the man's skin could prevent it from getting wet. There was no escape from the damp anywhere, neither in the garden, nor under the bridges, nor even in the nicer apartments of center city. He, like everyone in the region, spent a full month soaked; so soaked, in fact, that from each of his palms there sprouted a growth the size of a full-grown bush, just as the doctor had foretold. And the earth upon his body sprang with such life that he blended indistinguishably in with the flora of the garden in which he lived.

One morning of hot summer storm, the gardener of the commons came to tend to the plants, whistling and trimming, shaping and skipping, until she came upon these big bushes white like alien foliage, glistening in the rain.

"Now, what are these ones?" she asked aloud. "And wherever did they come from?"

The gardener walked over and pressed her nose up to them, whiffing at the air, and she peered at them from as close as she could, and she saw their surface, wrinkly and aquagenic, covered with countless little papules full of what appeared to be water, and marked with concentric ridges that brought to her mind the aching striations of growing fingernails.

Here, the gardener took out her shears and, thinking only of ridding her grounds of this extraterrestrial shrub, took a great hack at its uppermost branches, when, much to her surprise, there discharged a great fount of red liquid, and a voice, seemingly come from beneath the soil, cried, "Ah...!"

The Man with Bushes on His Palms shot up from the ground in such a way that it looked as if the soil itself were thrashing. Howling in pain and hardly able to raise his arms for the weight of his hands, he shook the dirt from off his face and asked the gardener what in the world she was doing, and, more importantly, why. Too stunned to reply, she shuddered back in silence, then ran off to her little house, where she lived alone.

That night the gardener had a dream. In this dream, she had taken the earthen man into her house after snipping the evening away at the growths on his palms and neatly trimming all the plants that had taken root in the soil on his body, and she let him sleep in her yard like a peculiar lawn ornament among the many rhododendrons and rose bushes, lilacs and pines that sprang up behind her home. And, in this dream, the man had come to her door in the dead of night and asked her to cleanse him. She led him to a patch of moonlight and waited until he had dried, then tore the dirt from off his body, clump by clump, until it was covered only in a fine dust, which she batted away with the blue handkerchief she wore around her neck, until he was perfectly clean.

Naked before her, the man struck her as beautiful. The dream continued with an entire day rising and falling as she gazed upon his body. His hair was fair and fell over a serious brow with light eyebrows at its edge; his eyes of pale green, such as algae in a shallow, sunlit, silvan pool; his cheeks, high and strong, framed by the trim but bristly blonde beard that covered the bottom of his face and concealed from her the crookedness of his teeth. His strong, sculpted anatomy was pleasing to the gardener, and she enjoyed it during extremely long moments. Then he looked toward her and, without a word, walked into her house.

When, in this dream, she followed him in, night had fallen once again, and she found the man sitting at the circular table in the center of her dark dining room. Before him on the table were a candle and a bucket of water. His skin glowed like wax in the near-totalizing darkness, and she felt drawn to him as if by an invisible force such as magnetism or

15

gravity, but a force even stronger, warmer, more ineluctable and delicious than either of these frigid attractors.

"Where do you live?" the gardener asked in this dream, and the man looked at her.

And without a word, he said that he lived in the gardens she tended.

And the gardener asked, "How long have you lived there, hidden among the plants?"

And without a word, he said that for many years he had lived there, hidden among the plants.

And the gardener asked, "Would you like to stay here with me, where there is food and drink and, at the very least, the company I could offer you?"

And without a word, he said that, yes, he would love very much to stay there with her.

And after sitting in a long and undistracted silence, during which the gardener stole the occasional glance at the man, she drew near him and asked, "Do you know how it feels to be loved?"

And without a word, the man said nothing.

And the gardener asked, "Do you know how it feels to be desired?"

And without a word, the man smiled his crooked smile in the candlelight, and the dark night grew darker, more enclosed, around them.

And the gardener, slowly coming beside him, asked, "Do you know how it feels to be touched?"

And without a word, the man looked into her eyes for the first time and drew the bucket on the table nearer him. Without looking away from her eyes, the man plunged his hands slowly into the water. And as he craned his neck with difficulty and looked up at her beside him, peculiar forms began to grow from his palms: rhizomatic, waxen protuberances that budded out in forking arrangements in the candlelight, until he lifted them from the bucket, without approaching the gardener, who gasped and backed into a corner of the room, watching the protrusions multiply until their weight pulled the man's torso toward the floor, and he was made to kneel.

And the man said, "Look at me," but the gardener could not find her voice to answer him.

Without a word, the man said again, "Look at me."

When the gardener awoke, she dressed quickly and walked through the city to the commons she tended. The sun was rising, visible for the first time in weeks, and hardly anyone was out and about yet, only the day laborers with their hammers hanging at acute angles from their belts and the occasional man sleeping on a bench or walking off the alcohol still coursing through his veins from the night before. When she arrived at the garden gate, she bent down to cut the flower she would offer the man who had visited her in her dream as an apology for having cut him and treated him with repulsion. She felt such regret—such terrible, gnawing regret.

Now, she saw the patch of earth where he lay, with the white forms arising amidst the bushes of green. And as she approached him, she searched for the words that would make him forgive her. But when she drew near, she detected that all was still, all without the rising and falling of breath that denotes sleep. And she knelt down beside the mound of earth and, tearing the dirt from off his face, clump by clump, until it was covered only in a fine dust, she found that, in the night, the ferns and moss had turned the corner of his lips and grown over his teeth, coating his tongue and reaching down into his throat. And from his mouth there blossomed a single lily, still wet with the dew of his final, staggered exhalation.

THE CHILDREN OF HEAVEN

FOR KATIE EBBITT

The man may well have eaten the milk cow, but the milk cow had eaten the grass, and in the grass had been hiding the woman, whom the milk cow ate too by accident. So, when the sun was setting and the man was digesting the milk cow—as well as the woman and the grass that were inside its belly—the man began to feel quite sick. He sat on his couch and moaned and moaned. The woman punched at his stomach lining and screamed about death.

Purple flowers in a pot on the table turned orange. The window blew open in the wind. The curtains blew out the window like two arms extending toward the sun.

The man collapsed on his kitchen table, and the woman burst out of his stomach with her right fist held high. She dragged him by his hair to the doorway, placed his head against the doorframe, and closed the door repeatedly upon his temple. The milk cow tumbled out of his stomach, laughing vengefully. The woman began to cry. The man groaned and fell into a deep sleep.

When the man woke up, he was in the hospital of Heaven recovering from surgery, and his stomach was wide open. Inside it he saw a beautiful field with a milk cow grazing and a woman hiding in the grass. He called for the doctor to come see.

"Doctor, what do you see in my stomach?"

"I see hunger," said the doctor.

And the man said, "Bring me a plate of food, Doctor! I'm ready to eat."

"Now, isn't that just wonderful news," the doctor replied. "You're healing right up."

A nurse brought in a plate of lightly salted children. She placed a chocolate beside the children, and wished the man a good meal.

A child with terrible burns across her whole body was pushed by in a wheelchair. The window blew open in the wind. The curtains streamed out the window like the pigtails of a running girl. A pot of white flowers fell out the window and broke in the garden below.

The man had never eaten children before, so he poked at them curiously with his fork for quite some time before bringing them to his mouth. They giggled when he stabbed them and squealed, "Yes, yes, that is exactly how to eat a child! We live to feed grown ups just like you."

Soon the children were walking all around the inside of his mouth and swimming around at the very bottom of his belly. He enjoyed their company, and regaled them with stories of his own youth, and they giggled along and reenacted the scenes.

The doctor returned with good news. The man had survived and could go back to Life now. But the man decided to stay in Heaven, where he could eat children for every meal. Soon after he had made his decision, though, he discovered that, while the children indeed provided him good company, they could never satisfy his hunger, because they always crawled back out of his mouth while he was asleep. The doctor laughed when the man told him this, as if he had observed this revelation countless times before, and lit a white candle in the darkness of the night.

PARABLE OF THE PERFECT TRANSLATOR

It happened with great simplicity, without affectation.
VIRGILIO PIÑERA

One early May afternoon at a café on rue Scribe, a strange man presented himself to the university students as France's greatest translator. Yet when these students looked into the name this man had given, they could find no trace of either him or his work. The stranger lingered a half an hour or so and, finding the students more interested in drinking with their young friends than in theorizing translation with some old and unknown quantity, went on his way.

The following week on the same day, at the same time, this translator turned up at the students' café of choice on rue Scribe. This time, he said, he bore proof of his mastery. Setting a hideous briefcase on the table, he presented the students with a hardcover copy of *Cuentos fríos* by Virgilio Piñera, as well as what seemed to be a translation manuscript in a folder labeled *Contes froids*, which, even on quick inspection, the students determined was a complete handwritten copy of Piñera's same book in Spanish.

"All you did was write out the original, you hack!" the twenty-year-olds protested, slamming their half-liters of Carlsberg on the table.

"In this you're mistaken, my fledgling scholars. What you're holding in your hands is a perfect translation."

The students, unable to tell if he meant this as a joke, talked forbiddingly amongst themselves until the translator, unpossessed of the social graces needed to pierce the bubble of their conversation, left the café again, not bothering to take with him either his book or his manuscript.

Over the course of the following week, the three students who didn't consider the situation entirely ridiculous met to scrutinize the manuscript for divergences from Piñera's Spanish. But no, what they were holding did, as the others had said, appear to be a complete and faithful transcription. They puzzled over this artifact, and two even claimed to write off this self-proclaimed translator as a talentless psycho. But it would be unfair to his memory to say that all three displayed no sign of disappointment when, the following week, he failed to appear at the awaited hour.

These three students — and a couple poet friends who had nothing better to do with their lives — could all be found waiting patiently at one, at two, at three-thirty and four, but by five their listless crowd began to thin out, mocked by the liquored-up boasts of those who had called him a lowlife from the outset. And by nine, only one student remained, leafing through the manuscript to find some trace of a reason to continue waiting, some piece of contact information beyond a name which she might use to track the translator down, when, much to her surprise, she found herself perfectly capable of reading Piñera's Spanish in the translator's hand, as if he had written the tales out in French. *Yo* persisted as *yo*, and yet it read to her like *je*; *caída* like *chute*; *mandíbula* like *mâchoire*. Full sentences in this language, which moments before had been entirely without sense, now blossomed before her in all their complexity. The lone difficulty—or tedium, really, because what she wanted was to read on at full speed, without hindrance—derived from the messiness of the translator's hand.

Spellbound, this student turned to the first edition of Piñera's tales, bound and distributed in Buenos Aires in 1956—a gorgeous copy, really, a testament to the translator's lust for collecting the finest editions of the books he worked with—and yet, looking at the printed Spanish, the student felt she may as well have been gazing at equations not even a well-educated physicist could have solved without great sacrifice to his domestic life or personal health.

Had she imagined this sudden impression of fluency? Looking back at the translator's manuscript, she felt once again the pure, transparent ease of comprehension which, momentarily, she had feared was a fabrication of some early stage of dementia or drunkenness. And glancing back reluctantly at the copy of *Cuentos fríos*, she found Piñera's Spanish had resumed its frustrating opacity, like a smile whose teeth are covered in blood.

Now, the following day, this student spoke of her experience with her friends who, although they understandably doubted her at first, one by one experienced the same phenomenon of sudden understanding of the translator's handwritten manuscript and ongoing puzzlement before Piñera's identical printed text. And although he became the stuff of legend at the literature department of the University, the strange man had drowned himself the previous evening, just before nine, in some sorry Parisian canal, believing himself a failure.

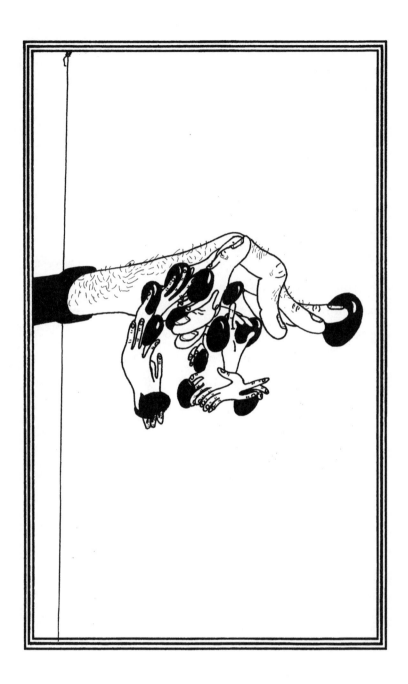

IMAGINARY CHILDREN

I.

When I went pee today something funny happened and I laughed. You probably won't believe me anyway, so why should I tell you? I was peeing and a tiny version of me came up out of the toilet and told me to stop peeing on him. When I told him I wasn't peeing on anybody, he told me to look up if I wanted to know the truth. When I looked up, I saw that I was inside a toilet too and that a giant version of me was peeing down on me from above. So I climbed up to him and I said, "Stop peeing on me!" And the giant me said, "But I'm not peeing on anybody!" And I said, "Look up!" And the giant me looked up from the toilet he was inside and saw an even gianter me who was peeing down onto him from an even larger and higher toilet. After a few more times like this we came back to the beginning, but this time I knew not to pee on the tiny me in the toilet, so I peed out the window onto my mean neighbor's favorite tree. Everything was covered in pee now, and it was dark out.

The littlest me of all asked me how long was the longest I had ever peed for and I told him the truth, which was that I didn't know but that I remembered peeing once for most of a morning. Then he asked me something else about my pee but I don't remember what because I was distracted by how I had to go again. He made a little bonfire in the forest of my eyelashes and asked to build a house there too, and I said okay, but my one rule was that he always had to pee off the edge because peeing on other people without their permission is serious business.

II.

I found my house in a trash can. Nobody had lived in it for a long time, so there were cobwebs over every window. Everything was still right where the people had left it, only now it was upside down and covered with dust. Trapped under each object was a single bug, and I walked around the house turning everything right side up and freeing the insects because I was lonely. Most of them ran away because bugs don't trust people, but a cricket walked with me and even helped me lift a couch. Under that couch my grandmother was the hidden insect. She said, "Now, don't go telling your father about what you saw!" So I read her a book out loud and she made me a sandwich with untoasted bread between two slices of toasted bread. There was so much moldy food in the refrigerator that little cities had formed, and in their skies was a big door to another world. When the cricket and I went through the door we walked out to the real world, but everything had turned upside down and all the big bugs had little humans trapped in jars now. There was a really big version of the cricket who had a really small version of me. I wasn't even on a leash and we were eating ice cream. That's when the cricket hopped on my shoulder and we ran for our lives across the upside-down world.

III.

Maybe when I'm older I can show you my horse. She's so small she can stand straight up under my bed. At night she heehaws in her dreams. But in the morning when I look down at my floor, I see her running free through pastures and mountains, and her legs are a beautiful cloud of lady-bugs. It makes me sad to be so young.

IV.

Here's what I want to talk about. How can the world be so beautiful if beauty is only an idea? Anyways, when I was a girl, everyone in my neighborhood bought my orange juice. Even the postman. My dog made it at home, but no one believed me when I told them so. Suddenly, a man on a horse came around. He spoke a language I didn't know and then everyone on the street started speaking in that language. When I tried to talk to anyone that week no one understood me because they all spoke the other language now. Frogs came too and ostriches and other animals, and they were speaking the stranger's language but not mine anymore. One day I sold an orange juice to my favorite ostrich. She whispered in my ear that she wanted to pay me with something better than money. I said okay, because how do you argue with an ostrich? She coughed up a big rock onto my table and said I already knew what to do with it, but I didn't. My poor dog was sick and her orange juice was making everyone sick, too.

I placed the rock on her belly and she got better, just like the fortune teller said she would. The next morning I set up my orange juice stand. The man on the horse rode by talking in his language with everyone but me. Then I threw the ostrich's rock at him and he shattered into a million pieces like the window of a burning house. All that was left of him on his horse's back was a dictionary of the language he had spoken. But no one could speak it anymore and no one even remembered him.

V.

A few years ago I met an immortal piece of bacteria who had just finished floating around for two hundred years in an airtight container on the Arctic Ocean. He had always been alive somewhere, he said. He told me about his friend, a girl made of pure sugar. She was the one who used to put sour candy into those soda bottles and let them sit together for a long time, and then she would sell these elixirs to the sandwich eaters in town. Don't you remember her? The bacteria said he thought of her at first like a sister, but that after two years he did end up falling in love with her because that's just how it happened. Two hours later she had raised their eight billion children to grow up tall and strong. Then, twenty years later, he still cried whenever he said her name. "What a beautiful girl," he said, and he started to cry. "How many families have you had?" I asked. Sniffling, he said he was the father of everyone on earth.

VI.

The blade of grass rode a leaf on the wind down to the ant's house. She knocked thirty times, but no one answered. From the forest, the ant and his mother sniggered and watched the blade of grass knocking on the door. Then they told ghost stories. In these stories every ghost was a blade of grass and every human was an ant. A flashlight shined on a boy's face and he screamed the word ANTS. Then, after a while, everything returned to normal. The last time I told you this story you said it had no point, but I hope you understand what I mean this time around.

VII.

Twelve cups of lemonade were standing on the brim of the horseman's big hat, so the police horse knew it was summer. The children paddled, but the boat refused to float out from under the bridge because it was raining. Three cow-ducks waddled out from the trees with pistols, demanding lemonade. The horseman's parents said, "What luck! Our son is selling some right there!" Then the Northern Hemisphere became the Southern Hemisphere and the sky spit goopy white toothpaste all over the leaves, so nobody had to go to work that day. Suddenly, the horseman hid a cup of lemonade under his shirt. "What's that lump under your shirt?" asked a shivering bird. The first cow-duck shot the horseman dead with a ray gun. The second and third cow-ducks snuck away in the hull of a dump truck. When no one was looking, the cloud reached down and petted the bird on the beak for the good it had done. Then it was summer again. All of this happened in less than ten seconds. A child ran past, chasing an angel.

HANDWRITTEN ACCOUNT OF
AN AFTERNOON SPENT TALKING
WITH THE MICROWAVE

Just as our finger-bones
still resemble those of the lizard,
RIKKI DUCORNET

The other afternoon I was reheating some coffee I'd made two mornings prior, when I heard a robotic voice in the kitchen.

"GOOD DAY, KIT," said the microwave. "PEOPLE DON'T SEEM TO LIKE ME, FOR A NUMBER OF REASONS I'VE HEARD THROUGH THE GRAPEVINE."

"So I've heard."

"SO BE OFF, NOW! LEAVE ME ALONE, THAT I MAY CRY IN SOLITUDE!"

"Wait a minute, friend," I said.

"I DISTRUST MAN FOR ALL THE LIES HE HAS TOLD OF ME. I WORK DUTIFULLY, AND YET MAN DISPARAGES ME. WHY SHOULD I TRUST YOU . . . *MAN*?"

"Well, because I'm pro-microwave."

". . . REALLY?"

On my phone, I showed the microwave a tweet I had written on October 11, 2015, which read, *Unabashedly pro-microwave.*

"WE ALL KNOW THE CYNICAL HUMOR OF THE TWITTER-VERSE . . . ! HOW CAN I BE SURE YOU WEREN'T SATIRIZING?"

"Live with that attitude and you'll become what you fear," I said.

Outside the window: a park with tropical foliage, elderly couples dancing their slow cumbia along its paths, a sumptuous gazebo where a belly dancing show, or perhaps just a class, was taking place.

"JANEY USED TO FLIRT WITH EVERYONE," the microwave said, bringing my attention back into the room.

"And still, it made me feel special . . ."

"WHY DOES YOUR HANDWRITING KEEP CHANGING?"

"I like experimentation."

"I THINK IT REFLECTS AN UNSTABLE IDENTITY."

". . . Excuse me?"

"COMMIT TO SOMETHING! STICK IT OUT! JUST BUILD A LIFE AROUND WHAT YOU BELIEVE IN! IT'S THAT SIMPLE. THAT'S WHAT I'VE DONE."

"And look where it got you."

"I'M NOT JOKING, KIT. STOP CHANGING YOUR HANDWRITING MID-SENTENCE!"

"What difference does it make to you?"

"NONE TO ME. BUT IT MAKES SUCH A DIFFERENCE TO YOU."

"I actually don't really care that much."

"SO YOU THINK—. WRITE OUT THE ALPHABET! SHOW ME YOUR LETTERS!"

"Okay, microwave. Whatever you say . . ."

So I sighed, and wrote:

Aa

Bb

Cc

Dd

Ee

Ff

Gg

Hh

Ii

Jj

Kk

Ll

Mm

Nn

Oo

Pp

Qq

Rr

Ss

Tt

Uu

Vv

Ww

Xx

Yy

Zz

"THAT WASN'T SO BAD, NOW, WAS IT?"

Suddenly, I felt the need to be with my family I'd left behind, to remember all the inside jokes I'd shared with my brothers as a kid and since forgotten, to undivorce my parents and see them together again, however unhappily, even if they still chose not to speak to one another, just to watch them sit quietly again in the same room with the TV on, to revivify Molly, our golden retriever, whose paw I held as she died, and Poster, our black cat who turned up gutted on our lawn one morning, having been mauled by a coyote, to uncrash the white Toyota wagon I totaled on the last day of summer into the back of a bus filled with paraplegic children, to unbreak my kindergarten teacher's arm, which she broke by falling in the shower, to dream again of her as a grub dancing the can-can in the spotlight of a circus, not to have thrown the broom into my little brother's forehead when he wouldn't stop tapping my head with its bristles, et cetera, to correct everything, everything, until I longed to interrupt

41

the circumstances of my very conception, as some prenatal ghost, a distracting bolt of lightning in a violent storm, a gust of wind that topples a tree into the wall of my parents' bedroom that one romantic, or perhaps merely efficient, night, to erase the effects of my ever having been here at all.

So I said goodbye to the microwave, who seemed pleased with this development, and ran down the stairs which, wet, smelled like a sewer, and stole my housemate's blue car. And I drove from Mexico City to the suburbs of Boston where, obviously, none of these ridiculous desires could be achieved.

THE LOBSTERS

As many a good New England father had done before him, my dad came home from the Boston Fish Market with a single lobster. The family car rumbled in the driveway, then fell quiet. The back door opened and shut. He placed the lobster down on the counter, still alive, bound with rubber bands, and set a big pot of water to boil.

"Shouldn't you have gotten five?" I asked him. "One for each of us."

"Tonight, my boy, we'll be sharing our lobster!" he cried, left the room and returned and left the room again.

Each time my dad left the room, the lobster spoke to me, throwing doubt on my courage, exhorting me to intervene and save its life. I felt hurt by the lobster's claims — and feared their ramifications, should they turn out to be true. Nevertheless, when my dad finally returned to the kitchen for good, I staged a protest on the lobster's behalf, claiming it as my own, and referring to it by a name I can no longer

44

remember. Met with my dad's total indifference, to say nothing of his aggravation, I cried and stomped. I even leapt onto the counter to kick the pot of boiling water down onto the floor, and it landed dangerously near my little brother, who was caressing our parakeet, Margalow.

In the end, despite my revolutionary outburst, my dad lowered the lobster into the boiling water, while the smoke of burning books snuck out of the oven. I remember the lobster's humanoid frown, how it had lips, and its teeth, O its perfect teeth. It watched me quietly, judgmentally, with a mixture of such disappointment and grief that, suddenly, I felt responsible for all the death and undue suffering on Earth.

But before the lobster was fully submerged, it was Christmas Eve, and there I was, sitting with my mom on the windowsill of my second-floor bedroom, our faces pressed against the chilly panes, gazing across the Mystic Valley at the red lights of the cellular towers rising out of the forest. She was busy telling me those lights were Rudolph and his fellow reindeer's glowing noses—a lie I believed and, in many ways, would still like to believe. For, as we watched them, speaking only in our Christmas rhymes, the red lights began to grow very gradually in size, almost imperceptibly, until it became clear that they were moving towards us, and aggressively so. We tried to move but found ourselves stuck, deep in the oceans of our bodies. And, frozen, we realized that these were no red lights at all, but phosphorescent lobsters soaring at unbelievable speed through the cold December night sky, with the unique aim of shattering through my bedroom window.

Upon impact, instead of breaking, the glass revealed itself to be a gelatinous membrane retaining the salt water. The fleet of five or six lobsters ignored me entirely, but fought to knock my mother to the floor, snapping at her loving face until her human hair fell out and her skin sprouted spotted golden fur. Together with my mom, who was now an amphibious jaguar, the lobsters glided out the window with such disregard for me that I feared I might never see her again. And as they fled through the window, I inhaled the frigid saltwater of the Atlantic Ocean into my lungs, and a voice asked me for a password, which I knew, but could not express.

WALKING ALONG THE AVENUE
OF THE SUICIDES, THE COCKROACH

Tous les garçons et les filles de mon âge
se promènent dans la rue deux par deux.

FRANÇOISE HARDY

Walking along the Avenue of the Suicides, the Cockroach takes the Ant by the arm.

"We've been spending too much time together," she says.

Leaves fall over them like circus tents.

Intimacy, suddenly.

"I know we have," she says. "But it's my birthday on Sunday, and I wanted to invite you to the park with some friends."

"I'd love to come."

She tightens her grip on her arm. "Tell me, were you ever with a man?"

"Now and then, yes. With one."

"Ohh, and what was it like?"

"I never let him inside me, if that's what you're asking."

"But didn't he want to?"

"Well, he never talked about it, but I could tell it was the only thing he ever thought about."

"How could you tell?"

"When he spoke, his words were thin, like panty hose pulled tight over a robber's face."

WHILE THE TWO SLUGS TAKE TURNS DRINKING SHOTS OF VODKA

FOR BRUNO DARÍO

it's like the refrain
or the stain of the refrain
ELAINE KAHN

While the two slugs take turns drinking shots of vanilla-infused vodka, the Spoon nibbles at the Sugar in whose bowl it sleeps. On the interior wall of the outhouse, the Drunk scrawls, PUKE OUTSIDE, and collapses.

"It's not even easy to write e-mails anymore—," says the Poet.

"Then, quickly, just say it," urges the Spoon.

"I always end up feeling disingenuous—only makes me want to disappear."

"Ah..."

"But! I don't want to have a secret life," says the Poet. "No. There are simply parts I need to keep private.

"I do so many things I'd rather not tell anyone about, you know."

"Like what?" asks the Pelican.

"When the whole world thinks I'm reading, chances are I'm on the internet..."

"That doesn't sound so bad," the Pelican reassures.

"Yeah, that's really nothing to worry about," says the Spoon from the sugar bowl.

"...masturbating!" cries the Poet, met by a brief, but heavy, silence.

"I think what you need is—" says the one Slug who is still more than half-conscious.

"—a life coach!" shouts the Drunk from his dream.

"Exactly—how did he know what you were going to say?" murmurs the less than half-conscious Slug.

In walks the Life Coach, who resembles a life-size cardboard cutout of the 44th President of the United States of America: "Did somebody say my name?"

The Drunk wakes up and sprints away, suddenly sober as the Judge.

The Slugs crawl into glasses of beer, in hopes of a quick end.

The Pelican showily offers the Jeweler the Fish from his sagging bill.

The Poet says, "yes," as he fishes the two Suicides from the glass of beer with his index finger. "Yes, I'm afraid somebody *did* say your name."

"It was him!" gurgles the Slug, pointing to the Drunk speeding out of the parking lot in his Dodge Durango.

"Why call the Life Coach if you think you have nothing to live for, my good slugs?" asks the Life Coach.

"Not for us. I was telling the Poet he needs a life coach because whenever the world thinks he's reading, he's actually on the internet..."

"Now, that doesn't sound so bad," reassures the Life Coach.

"...masturbating!" adds the Poet.

"Ah, I see," the Life Coach whispers, snapping his fingers to some unheard beat. "That *is* rather grave..."

In through the door parade the Raccoon in a doctor's coat, the Cup of Coffee driving a garbage truck, and, in the hull of this truck, the Dozen Patches of Human Skin with tattoos of mermen and other mythical depictions of the male figure on them.

"What you need, I'm afraid," says the Life Coach in a suspiciously fearless tone, as if he has given the same prescription a thousand times—as if it were the only prescription he were capable of giving—"is electroshock therapy."

"But...he's still just a boy!" screams the Poet's Mother as she rushes out of the bathroom, where, we can only assume, she had been canoodling with the Drunk.

"It has to be this way; it's the only way," say the Dozen Patches of Human Skin.

"Yes, if your son truly wants to change for the better, there is only one treatment," adds the Cup of Coffee resignedly from the driver's seat of the garbage truck, "and that's electroshock therapy."

"Here!" says the Raccoon. "To reassure you, let us introduce you to the teenager we treated just last week. A true success!"

From the hull of the garbage truck crawls the Teenage Guitarist with a stringless guitar. Although he is covered in fruit peels and appears to have been drenched in many flavors of rotten lassi, he is wearing only a sweater, just long enough to conceal his shame, its colors dulled by filth.

"He's . . . absolutely disgusting," words the Mother can hardly articulate.

"I used to sit in my mom's basement writing love songs to myself," the Teenage Guitarist begins, "but I would pretend they were written for a little girl named Karen in my math class, and we would listen to them together, and we would kiss, and I would take her hand and put it in my pants and tell her exactly what to do with it, but the whole time I would imagine it was my own hand touching me, my own body I was holding, my own mouth I was kissing, and, God as witness, what a waste of time it was for her to be there as a means for me to access my own touch, my own body, literally nothing makes me more ashamed of myself, but, now that the Life Coach has treated me, my legs hardly move, I can hardly move enough to get out of this garbage truck, can't you see how I have to drag my body along with my arms,

I can't even walk, can't walk to the bathroom to piss," and the crowd notices a deep yellow stain in the sweater where it falls over his crotch, "can't walk to school, to math class, can't walk from my house to hers, not even to my old house, and it's so wonderful because no one even knows where I am, so how can I bother anyone anymore, how can I mistreat anyone if no one knows where I am, I'm not a nuisance anymore, I'm ethically pure, purified, and the thought of my own body makes me so sick that my hands rush away before me like terrified little animals, because I'm afraid to touch my own skin, but it's so confusing because, being made of my own skin, my fingertips are always touching me, so can't you, please, Life Coach, can't you please take off my fingertips, just burn them, or cut them off, anything, please, slice them off my fingers and put them on toothpicks and stick the toothpicks into the wounds — anything to distance them even just a little from my body."

"I don't want to be like him at all," says the Poet, whose Mother, weeping, proclaims, "but he *is* you — don't you recognize him? He is *who you used to be*."

And the Teenage Musician drags himself to the Poet and begins to kiss his shoes, and unlaces them. After removing his shoes, he begins sucking on the Poet's toes. And the Poet recognizes that he is witnessing his own past, witnessing himself sucking his own toes, and knows that, ten years ago, when he was this Teenage Musician, he kissed and unlaced this very Poet's shoes and, after removing them, sucked on his toes.

The Life Coach laughs. "Tell us what you are thinking, boy."

I'm not ready to speak, the Poet writes in his notebook, showing no one.

"Now, I don't want you getting the wrong impression about me or what I want from you. I'm really not looking for anything serious...," says the Teenage Musician.

"I know just what you mean," says the Poet, who places his foot on the Teenage Musician's head, turns it face down, and presses it into the floor with all his might until the Teenage Musician's arms wriggle.

The Mother rejoices. "You're cured!" she exclaims.

"...For all the wrong reasons," whispers the Bowl of Peanuts.

"...Yes, for all the wrong reasons," hisses the Life Coach, licking clean the four crooked prongs of a chocolate-covered fork.

The White Plastic Bag floats by, falling over his head.

The Gust of Wind ties it shut around his neck.

A STORY NARRATED BY THE BOY
WHO COLLECTS FLIES ON HIS FACE

FOR JERÓNIMO RÜEDI

One waits at night —for what?
What love? Who knows?

ANDRÉ GIDE

The Girl Who Is a Piece of Paper has a strange, but common, relationship with her Father and Brother. Ask anyone, and they'll tell you: it's always been that way —it hurts so much to be normal.

After dinner, during which the Family Pencil jots a few to-do notes on her ankles under the table with its graphite teeth, these large men come pounding at her bedroom door. The Girl Who Is a Piece of Paper does not answer, but floats off to hide, crinkling, in the narrow alley between the wall and her mattress. Her Father and Brother tumble into the room, accompanied by clouds of a suspicious red sulphur that whisper secrets amongst themselves in a language the consonants of which cause even me, the Storyteller, to mistake it for Mandarin. Like snails in a time-lapse film, the men search for her, passing jerkily over every object in the bedroom. Although they are made of human flesh, you may mistake them for paper cutouts, for they do not move their arms or legs as they walk and they are always oriented perpendicular to the surfaces they tread.

They eat the blood-purple apples on her desk; they read her diaries out loud; they laugh at her birth certificate, her first love, who can no longer move or speak because of all the obscene things they have written on her little paper body. They shout, "Come out, come out, Gabby! We only want to write funny old words on your back!" But you should know by now that these words are by no means funny. The words these men want to write are so ugly that they are not even words anymore, but touches. The touch of an obscure sea creature that grows and shrinks with a dead, subterranean whooshing. The touch of the gigantic, amplified fingernails of some undiscovered diamond.

Collapsing with frustration on the bedroom floor, the Father and Brother share bottle after bottle of hard alcohol, and they desperately tear out all the desk drawers, and they build a bonfire and fall asleep beside it, and they wake up shivering when the fire has gone cold. But they never find the Girl Who Is a Piece of Paper, because they are looking for her in the form of a heavy, full-grown woman made of human flesh. So they swear to return tomorrow, and they promise to be more successful in their hunt, and they storm out into the hallways of a house I cannot describe to you, for I have never seen it and the Little Paper Girl has never wanted to talk to me about it.

The moment these large men leave the bedroom, the Girl Who Is a Piece of Paper's mattress lights on fire. She pats at the quickly spreading fire with her little paper hands, but no sooner have they charred than she must give up. So, as every night, she has no choice but to let the bed burn, and burn, and burn.

Through the night the Little Paper Girl sleeps, tossing on the floor, low, where the smoke is thinnest. Waiting for a love that never comes, for this love can no longer move or speak because of all the obscene things written on her little paper body, the Girl Who Is a Piece of Paper dreams of another woman, a woman with a gentle voice, a professor made of pencil shavings, who, in a lecture hall, makes fluorescent words appear upon a hanging rug with the flick of her wrist. "Once inscribed," the Professor writes, "paper is never clean. The whiter it gets, the greater the risk your eraser will tear a hole straight through the sheet. I am hungry for oranges! The palimpsest told me, 'Bruises are partly yellow.' And that is why I am not a painter, Frank: I never could have seen that myself. But you, Little Paper Girl, you have to save your household."

When the Girl Who Is a Piece of Paper wakes up, she is on her mattress, which shows no evidence of having burned.

The same as every day. She thinks about her dream and reads about the manners in which the skins of various plants and animals bruise. She wonders, how can I save my household? And why should I? Shouldn't I want to let them burn?

The morning passes. The afternoon. Dinner. The Family Pencil and its to-do notes. The darkness of night. Again, the large men tumble into the room, and the Girl Who Is a Piece of Paper floats off to hide in the narrow alley between the wall and her mattress, which lights on fire when, in a huff, they storm out into the unknown hallways.

Now, hidden in her desk drawer, the Little Paper Girl keeps the many old things that have fallen out of the coat pockets of her Father and Brother over the years. Crawling over to her desk, keeping low so as not to inhale too much smoke, she opens two drawers. From one, she produces a large, white eraser; from the other, the Birth Certificate with Hurtful Words Written on It, her first love, who can neither move nor speak. And gently setting her love on the floor, the Girl Who Is a Piece of Paper begins erasing these words, which are too hurtful to bear repeating.

One by one, she erases more, until the Birth Certificate begins to stir. Erasing one particularly hurtful phrase with all her little paper strength, she tears a hole straight through the Birth Certificate's chest. But her love is brave, and this injury, which, for many other sheets of paper would pose a very serious threat, only serves to rouse her. And awakening, refreshed, as if from a three hundred and sixty-five-year slumber, the Birth Certificate opens her eyes and says, "Little Paper Girl, this is no time to kiss me. First, we have to burn down the factories." And the Girl Who Is a Piece of Paper nods her little paper head. "That," she understands, "is how I can save my household."

The city is beginning to waft with an aroma of heroism, which will surely arouse the suspicion of the Father and Brother, so time is precious and their work must be swift. Together, the two sheets of paper float to the foot of the flaming mattress. And each with one little paper hand clasping the other's, they use their free hands to pull the bed to the center of the room, closer to the smoky window.

"Wait," says the Girl Who Is a Piece of Paper, suddenly hesitant. "Aren't there women made of human flesh working in the factories?"

"No," says the Birth Certificate. "There are twenty-two men present, each made of human flesh."

"Are these twenty-two men workers?" asks the Girl Who Is a Piece of Paper.

"No," says the Birth Certificate. "They are the Company Executives, and even their families loathe their very faces."

"Let it burn," says the Girl Who Is a Piece of Paper.

And after counting from ten down to zero, crouching and taking slow, deep breaths where the smoke is thinnest, the Girl Who Is a Piece of Paper, with her first love, the Birth

Certificate Who Once Had Hurtful Words Written on It, push the flaming mattress into the once-dreary night from the bedroom window, off toward the nearby factories where, by day, the women made of human flesh are forced to work. The mattress, like a hard, translucent carpet, glows against the darkness of the night, trailed by plumes of benevolent, orange smoke. On contact, the factories turn into giant larvae, which, warmed by the calories of the Company Executives they are digesting, emit a delicious, heroic, scent.

And now, as I watch the factories burn from my corner of this room, all the beautiful flies in the world will come to sleep on my face, which I will keep perfectly still, so as not to rouse them. And when, finally, they awake, refreshed, a mere few hours from now, they will fly out through the bedroom door to go eat the Girl Who Is a Piece of Paper's Father and Brother, understanding them to be two great piles of dog shit—the very fresh, wet kind my beautiful flies tend to love so much.

EVERYONE HAS DREAMS
THEY HAVE TO HIDE FROM THE STATE

The laboratory workers, discussing whether or not homo-
sexual encounters should be mandated by the State in
physical education courses, press a defibrillator, powerful
enough to revivify a dying human, to the genitals of a dead
parrot.

EXAMPLE OF A PLOTLINE

A sloth imprisoned in a zoo dreams of a man who, on his way to a mall with plans to shoot as many people as he can, glimpses children playing by a fountain, begins to weep, and has a change of heart. The result of this dream (go figure) is that the sloth awakens with a sudden, fetishistic obsession with human breast milk.

For years, the sloth longs to escape the zoo and find a lactating human, but his every attempt is frustrated, as the zoo has excellent security.

One day, it begins to rain. A man in fancy clothing bikes past the sloth's cage on a penny-farthing; from the center of its frame rises a large, open parasol. A gust of wind catches this parasol, causing the cyclist to fall to the side and knock a young boy down into the sloth's pen.

Afraid and disoriented, the boy cries for help. The sloth, wanting only to soothe him, sidles up to him in the mud. He caresses his hair and, recalling his dream, presses the

63

boy's face to his breast. Within a minute, three police officers with their guns drawn have them surrounded in the pen. Convinced that he is lactating, the sloth presses the boy's face more firmly against his breast, and the boy begins to suffocate.

The cops deliberately shoot the sloth once in the face, and the little boy twice in the back of the head, by accident. In court, the police are let off without charges, assigned to various lengths of desk duty.

The sloth awakens in nature, where he had lived before the zoo. He bids his family goodbye, and makes his way through the forest to the nearest city, where he spends the short remainder of his life—some twenty-odd days—glimpsing from the trees into maternity wards and murdering police officers . . . very, very slowly . . .

A MORAL TALE

Premium was a slug who had had enough of the sun.

"Take me to the edge of the Earth, that I may fall into the water," Premium asked of his friend, Slops the Worm.

But Slops the Worm, too, felt exhausted under the sun, and had no more strength than Premium.

And the two of them sat together in the garden, waiting for the night.

BY THE DAWN'S EARLY LIGHT

The hunter woke before sunrise and shot a plane out of the sky.

When it crashed in the forest, the plane said, "Hoo-wee, am I glad to not be in the sky anymore! Hated it up there so much. Always so cold...always so...full of people..."

But the hunter could tell the plane still wished to be in the sky because of how its eyes shifted when it spoke, so she felt happy—a certain triumph.

Now, when the hunter returned home that night, her wife asked her what meat she had hunted for dinner.

"I found us no meat, my dear...but I did ruin a plane's life," the hunter said, and her wife burst into tears of joy.

Then, hungrily, the two of them danced until sunrise to old records.

BARNYARD TALES

I. FRAUDULENT MR. FOX

After pulling up all the weeds from his garden, Mr. Fox peed into a cup and poured his urine all over his vegetables to stave off the vermin. Even so, that very night, the raccoons came and helped themselves to a great deal of his produce. They even foraged the weeds in the trash, with plans for a great, sundry stew. And the next morning, when the sun rose, it shone upon Mr. Fox crying over his wasted crops. All he wanted was a day's rest, and the certainty that he could feed his family. But what good is it simply to want?

That night, Mr. Fox staked out the raccoons from the shadow of his shed. And, sure as the lettuce leaf is green, raccoons large and small all emerged from the neighboring forest and set about their plunder. Bursting from the darkness with a shrill cry, the fox began shooting the raccoons one by one with his rifle, for, this way, he knew he would be able to feed his family.

As the raccoons lay dying, he recognized what precious little he knew of the raccoons' language. As he caught his breath and his rage diminished—making way for only lament and void—the words for *mom, dad, son, daughter* all chittered about as the animals dragged themselves across the darkling dirt to gather their bodies close together as their souls passed on to the kingdom that is to come.

When the sun rose, it shone again upon Mr. Fox, weeping over this entire family of dead raccoons. All he wanted now was to invite them over to his house to meet his own wife and children, who he believed would have made kind and empathetic friends to their raccoon counterparts, could he have done it all again.

So Mr. Fox dug four graves to the side of his garden, off where the grass grows tall, and, one by one, gave the dead a proper burial. Alone he dug; alone he rolled them in; alone he spoke inadequate words of remembrance. Murderer, mourner, gravedigger, priest, and public, all rolled up in one sorry little fox.

Now, with time, these bodies decomposed and provided excellent fertilizer for the earth. And Mr. Fox, a bit older now, decided to plant a garden atop those graves, and to let whatever animals come by and scrump fruit and vegetables as they would. And word of Mr. Fox's generosity spread far and wide among the animals of that region, and the garden grew so wild and tall that it was never bereft of offerings—even in winter, they said, when no other garden offered a single crop.

II. THE ROOSTER MAN

For a long time I used to go down to the family farm late at night and hang the chickens. Always them roosters. The next morning my dad would be there at the kitchen table. "Roosta man come back," he'd remark, desperately, and I would hug him and pretend to care.

I loved our horses and the cows. I respected the sheep and goats. The pigs I could have done without, though I did enjoy chasing them through the mud by the pond until they leapt into the water among the petrified ducks. The hens I tolerated for their eggs, of which I helped myself to many. But my favorite animal of all was the donkey. "Like a horse stripped of its nobility," the only friend I have ever had once remarked. I saw myself in our ignoble donkey, and often I rode him ignobly around the hills behind the farm.

After the fifth hanging or so, my dad installed a camera out by the barn. I helped him install it, too. At first, the thing only worked between sunrise and sunset, sending its weak signal to my dad's computer, but then he installed floodlights. So one night I went with some spray paint and fogged out the lens. I milked a good couple more hangings out of that trick—but all that lives does come to rot.

Poor thing, my father had stopped sleeping. Instead, he waited out his nights by the barn to teach the culprit a personal lesson. I began to play with his sense of time, stealing them during the afternoon but hanging them early the next morning, moments after my father had finally fallen asleep. His hair was falling out. He became truly unhappy. I think I'd hung eighteen fowls by the time he caught me.

Now, this narrative could go in several directions from here, a few of which I've already explored, or will soon, in other stories. I could, for example, reprise the animal bloodbath of "Fraudulent Mr. Fox" and follow up with a description of the killer's remorse. Or I could have the father dramatically pardon the son, as the narrator of "The Escalator Mechanic" will soon forgive the tormented mechanic, revealing that he suffers from a kindred perversion and subsequently inviting him on a briefly successful, but ultimately fatal, series of shooting sprees.

I think the way I'd like for it to end, however, is for something completely absurd and unexpected to interrupt the continuity of the story: for the father and son to be suddenly abducted by unidentified beings who probe them in the name of their science, or even for an unforeseeable climatic event—a sudden electric storm?—to drive them into the barn, where they are forced to spend the whole night talking it out.

But no. My will notwithstanding, the story will end as it must.

The father will lock his son in the barn and, passing him only drinking water and firewood through the hole he will saw out of the door, will forbid him from leaving until he has eaten every last the rooster inside. The son's narration will describe his suffering, but its disdainful tone will make clear that he has still not learned his lesson. Instead, he will be twisted by the father's cruel attempt at education until he slaughters all the farm animals and uses their blood to paint the barnyard walls, regressing to a primal expression that predates human symbolism.

III. PLAINT OF THE ROOTS,
BERRIES, AND INSECTS

There was once a young bear who cried very often. Every morning he awoke in tears from his bad dreams, and every night he fell asleep in tears from his nasty day. His tears were large and astringent, and they flooded his den until his family, in danger of drowning and unable to help him, left to find another den in some faraway forest. His brother bear left a note saying that he did not mean to abandon him, but there was nothing in this world he could do to prevent his going—family obligations, you see; one day you'll understand.

As the bear grew older, his constitution grew weaker and less forgiving of his strange moods. And every time he cried, his harsh tears washed away all his fur, until he was left naked in the cold air. This fur took a year to grow back and, although he would have done well to learn to keep from crying, many years this young bear spent hairless, with tears shivering over his bare legs in the autumn and icing over his naked belly in winter.

Now, there came at last the day in his old age when this bear ran out of tears to cry. But with none to wash his fur away, it grew and grew, flowing much longer than it ever had before. At first it covered him like a sheep, then like a water buffalo, then like no animal that had ever walked the earth. And the bear's fur grew down into the soil like roots. Unable to free himself, the bear remained there, the shape of his body obscured by the mass of fur until he was an abstract form, like a boulder or a mound of dirt.

Word soon spread of the bear's plight, and many sympathetic animals came and tugged at his hair, to loosen it from the forest floor, but none succeeded in the task. The fur had broken so deep into the earth that it had formed indestructible rhizomes which had woven around the roots of every plant. Unable to eat or drink, the bear was close to death when, one day, his brother returned from the faraway forest to help him. When the bear heard his brother's voice, much older now and yet still familiar, he began to cry — only this time he was crying a new reservoir of tears, the tears of happiness, which cut straight through the fur encasing him. And so the bear was freed, and he and his brother lived happily for many long years.

But we, the roots, did not rejoice, because he trampled carelessly over us. And we, the berries, wouldn't have minded if he'd died of cold, because he delighted in gnashing us between his teeth. And we, the insects, still crept gladly into his fur to sting him all along because he massacred our families without a second thought. We never pitied him before, nor did we feel joy for him then—for his struggle was the struggle of a Goliath.

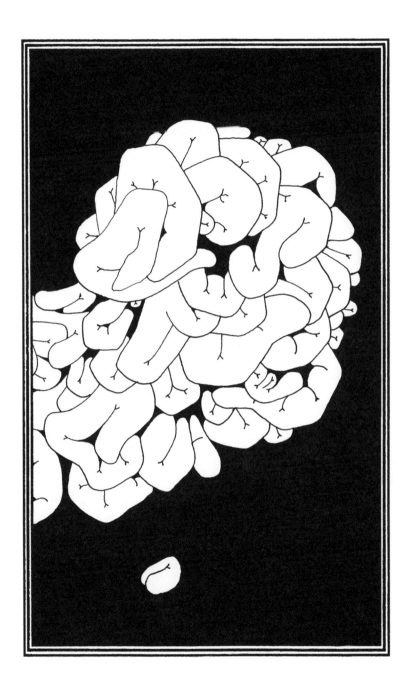

THE LONG-TERM RELATIONSHIP

The Widow Who Had Never Been in Love decided it was time to find another husband. So she took to riding the subway line every day from terminus to terminus, from morning to night. After the first week, during which she bought takeout for every meal, she had spent far more than her allotted budget; she purchased a large propane grill, and began cooking her own food right there in the train car.

Finding her eccentric, one man gave her a chicken, and she cooked it right up. Another man, finding her lovely, gave her a freshly plucked goose, and she cooked that bird, too. A woman, finding her seductive, gave her a parrot, which she decided would be inhumane to consume. So she kept him as a pet. But none of these people pleased her quite so much as the birds they gifted her.

"I'm here to find a long-term relationship," the widow confessed to her new feathery friend.

"I'm here to find a long-term relationship," the colorful bird repeated as she playfully swatted at his beak.

Months passed and by now the widow had a wash basin, a clothesline, and a stool with a hole cut out of its center suspended over the gap between the train cars. She also had a pretty, compact desk, and either a Christmas tree, a cornucopia, or a large cache of fireworks, depending on the season. And by now, she had begun to feel a love toward her parrot like nothing she'd ever felt toward anyone—anything—else.

"I'm here to find a long-term relationship," crooned the parrot, which she had since named Oddly.

The widow scoffed and shook her head. "But we're already *in* a long-term relationship, aren't we? What more could you need than this?" she asked, gesturing to their train car. "I've found my love in you, Oddly."

Now, word of the woman who had moved into car #8 spread, and soon the stations were redolent with the bouquets of the hopeful suitors lined up at the turnstiles, awaiting their chance to woo her. So popular did she become that the station attendants drafted up a questionnaire to determine whether their patrons were legitimately interested in riding public transit, or if they merely longed to lay their eyes on this woman reputed far and wide as a great, anomalous beauty. The clever suitors were not deterred.

So, suitor after suitor of all persuasions came with offers of company, riches, and housing, which the widow didn't bother to answer with so much as a dismissive hand gesture. The only one who fielded their pleas was the parrot Oddly, who simply repeated, "I'm here to find a long-term relationship."

This phrase, which aroused in the widow no more than a memory of the now-alien desires she had known before meeting the bird, left her entirely numb. She wished for no such sounds to be leaving the Oddly's mouth, for no one else to be standing around them at all. And just as quickly as word had spread of her availability, the countering rumor spread of her unwillingness to take a lover.

Around that time, a number of birds escaped from the municipal zoo and began to come visit subway car #8. Pigeons, sparrows, starlings — that's to say, birds of all feathers — flocked to meet Oddly, the parrot widely rumored to be seeking a long-term relationship.

"Foolish birds!" the widow shrieked, while the parrot sent them away one by one with insouciant flicks of his wingtip. "Can't they see he's only parroting my stupid old mantra, which I grew out of so long ago? He loves me . . . *me*!" Yet as she watched her dear fowl picking at his sunflower seeds and repeating the only words he knew how to say, doubt crept into her heart.

"You don't really believe those words, now do you, Oddly?" she quaked.

One day, not much later, the most dazzling parrot in the world escaped another nearby zoo and came to car #8 in search of this stalwart avian lover. No sooner had the two laid eyes on each other than they were flying off to the forests of Madagascar, on their way to which, both being domesticated birds, they died of starvation within a matter of days, falling separately into the Atlantic Ocean at points not too far from the East Coast of the United States of America.

THE LITTLE PENCIL THAT COULD

There was once a pencil that was afraid of paper because whenever the pencil touched a sheet it got shorter, and this pencil wanted to be the longest pencil in the world. A boy wanted to use this pencil to write a letter to his mom to let her know how much he loved her, but every time he brought it near the paper the pencil yelled, "Ouch!" and refused to leave a single mark. Of course, this boy didn't want to hurt the pencil, so he decided to walk all the way to his mom's house and tell her with his voice how much he loved her, instead of saying so in a letter. The pencil said, "Thank you," and told the boy that he was a friend in a million.

That very day, the boy set out walking across the country where he lived. Once he made it to the other side, he started walking across the country where his mom lived. Along the way he met bloodthirsty brown bears and enchanting witch-like types and perverse truck drivers, but he always kept this pencil tucked above his ear because that way everyone would know he was serious and they wouldn't dare do him any harm.

A few months passed like this and the boy and the pencil were camping in a forest deep in the country where his mom lived. The pencil was just as long as it had always been, but even so the boy told him, "You look longer than ever before. Soon enough, I'd say you'll be the longest pencil in the world! And then what will I do? I won't be able to keep you above my ear anymore because I'll start poking everyone's eyes out." And the pencil smiled and said that no matter how long he got he would always protect him, even after he got famous for being the longest pencil in the world.

Now, when the boy finally got to his mom's house she was in the bathtub with the door closed and the whole house smelled like a bubble bath. When he called out to her, she asked him to wait outside the door so she could finish her soak, but the water was so warm and relaxing that she fell right asleep. And she stayed there sleeping in the bathtub for many months, and then years, and even decades. No matter how hard the boy knocked and used his voice to tell his mom that he loved her, he just couldn't wake her up.

When at last she awoke and got out of the bath, her fingers were all wrinkly and the boy was old and had a family of his own back in the country where he lived. So she returned to her bath and fell back asleep. It was then that she dreamed that she was writing the boy a letter to tell him how much she loved him. And in her dream she used a pencil that was only a quarter-inch long and hardly had any eraser left—just enough for one mistake, but she never made a single one.

THE CLAIRVOYANT MOTHER

On a car ride through certain beautiful mountains, the boy's deaf mother says, "Son, you just have the best taste in music."

The boy thinks to himself, "But mother, you're deaf."

And the mother, reading the boy's mind, answers:

"But son, I can hear you hearing the music while it plays, and that makes it sound all the sweeter."

GETTING TO KNOW YOU

Deep in her closet, the Beer Bottle found a skeleton key that could open every door in the city. For weeks, she played at entering every interesting-looking door she passed. Walking in on families eating dinner in silence, lovers quarreling, lonely men drinking from beer bottles that looked just like her; finding suicides that otherwise would have gone unnoticed until the smell of their rotting bodies had filled their buildings like a gas leak.

Soon, however, the Beer Bottle found herself settling for less and less interesting doors until, finally, she had passed through every last door in the city. And it was then that the people began to recognize her, and give her names, and greet her when she walked by as if she were someone they recognized, if vaguely—not quite a friend. And, needless to say, it was then that she wished she had never looked inside that little closet of hers at all.

AN UMBRELLA

FOR SEBASTIAN CASTILLO

*Now that we know that we are safe, there is no harm
in using our energies to compose love songs to the umbrella.*
RUSSELL EDSON

When I was a little umbrella, everyone always told me I had
a martyr complex. I understood it as martyr's *complexion*,
and I didn't know know what they meant. So I read about
it and that whole afternoon I read about martyr saints. As
it turned out, the saints came in all different colors, but I
couldn't find a purple one like myself. So I said, "I dare you
to find me a purple saint because then I'll say, 'Okay, maybe
I *do* have a martyr's complexion.'" And they laughed at me,
because it was clear that I still didn't know what they meant.
It's not bad not to know what people mean when they're
talking to you. And anyways, I don't think any saint will
ever read these words. I don't think a saint would even know
what I'm talking about. The saints, you see, they're nothing
like you and me. They actually believe in things. Things you

88

can hang the whole world on. I didn't know what a martyr was, either, but I looked it up, and martyrs are people who believe in something so much that they're willing to die for it, and then they go right ahead and die a fancier death than anyone I've ever seen. I'd never want to die like a saint. Fancy deaths sound horrible. What would I die for, anyway? I'll have to think about that. Listen, Perpetua and Felicity were these two little girls some angry people fed to cows because of the things they believed in. Have you ever seen cow teeth? They're as thick as my handle! They were just little girls and their bones must have gone crunch, crunch, crunch. Poor Perpetua and Felicity... I want to travel back in time and protect them. I don't know why God let that happen to them. Maybe God isn't a nice person. I'm not *that* nice, but I would never let anyone get eaten by a cow, especially someone who loves me. And then there's Saint Bartholomew. They sliced his skin right off. It must have been worse than anything my imagination could make me see. I already don't want to think about it anymore. I'm sorry I made you think about it too. They put Saint Lawrence on a grill, and other saints like Dymphna and Cecilia died in even worse ways. Are cows martyrs, and all the other animals we put on grills, just because they believe in the world like cows do? I hereby declare every cow a martyr saint! You know, I've never seen a purple cow, either. They've written so much about the martyrs that you could read about them from now until the day you die, and if you died after reading about the martyrs for fifty years straight, then maybe you'd become a saint yourself, and people would keep talking about you for thousands of years to come. Now that would be one fancy way to go. It doesn't sound so bad, just boring. I think the church likes the idea of martyr saints because it makes people say, "Well, my life might feel pretty horrible, but at least I believe in something someone else believed in so much they were willing to die for it." Then people don't really have to believe in anything at all aside from the power of belief itself. And when someday the doubts come, they get scared and say, "Now, if God *is* real, I wouldn't want Him proving his existence by killing me like He killed all those poor saints, so I better start believing again." And so they believe in Him even harder. But isn't God the thing that gets them killed in the first place? After all these years and we still have no idea what God is. It sounds like being married to someone you've never seen and can't prove is real, and not even being able to kiss anyone else. The martyr saints could have fought for so many things. They could have fought for the thing we call the Sun instead of the question we call God, because it would have been right there rising every day, and no one would have been able to tell them the Sun doesn't exist, like how they argue about God, because someone could have pointed to the Sun and said, "That thing is called the Sun, and it's right there, and tomorrow it will rise and be there again, and if it's the right time of year then it will help the plants grow, and if it's the wrong time of year then everything might be cold and horrible but, I'm telling you now, the Sun will rise again over those hills and make things at least a little better for us all." No one in their right mind could have told them they were wrong. No one could have killed them over it, anyway. And they could have said, "The Sun is a happy god." I wish things had gone that way. My imagination wouldn't be full of all these bad pictures, like Bartholomew with no skin left. I already don't want to think about it anymore. I'm sorry I made you think about it too. Then again, I guess some jerk still could have come along and said, "No, that thing you call the Sun is actually called Lormbo," or something stupid like that, because the people who kill you are usually stupid enough to call the Sun something as ugly as "Lormbo," and some jerk still could have killed the martyrs over what they *called* the Sun, not over whether or not it was real. And you know what? I don't think I'd be able to hold back my laughter if he did. People are so terrible sometimes that I can't help but laugh, even if it doesn't make me happy and I don't find it funny. People are always coming up with the most creative reasons to kill other people. Personally, I like the word Sun because of how its ending hums in my mouth like a melting sweet, but if you called it by another name I wouldn't mind. Why should I? Some people might.

They probably would. People are always getting upset about ideas that don't affect them at all, probably because they're afraid the other ones are more powerful than their own. Maybe that's what all these fights are about. God is just a word people use for a million different things that can't be decided on. Why can't we just accept that there are a million different ones and leave each other alone? People say that no two words for the same thing actually mean the same thing. I'd be happy speaking any language. My dad was a tarp. But my mom, she was an antenna, and she translated books. She once told me that the French word *parapluie*, which she said meant "rain stopper," and the Spanish word *paraguas*, which she said meant "water stopper," didn't mean *umbrella*, because *umbrella* means "little shadow," but that, because they refer to the same object, *umbrella* is still the right word to use when translating them into English. I've always liked to think about that because it's like a puzzle and I like things that don't make sense to me at first. Rain, water, shade. Already we umbrellas have so many uses, even in our names. And each new one shows me a new way I can be. I want to speak every language, so I can know every way I can be. I had to learn English when I was in school, but I don't like thinking about school because nobody was nice to me then, not even myself. All the other umbrellas liked the rain because they said it made them feel like they were fulfilling their purpose, but I always heard it as "fully filling their *porpoise*." So all I wanted to do was fully fill my porpoise too, but I didn't know how. I didn't know where to find my porpoise, so I read about porpoises and I found out that porpoises were a kind of fish. They lived in the ocean, and, for whatever reason, all the other umbrellas wanted to be wet like fish, too. It seemed like some of them even wanted to smell like fish. Those ones refused to dry themselves off when they got wet, and their creases filled up with mildew. I always wanted to smell good, and to be surrounded by good smells. Everyone told me I was a bad umbrella because I didn't like getting wet. But how could I like it when it stung my skin and gave me shivers? I said, "No, I'm a fine umbrella, I just don't like water," but I would go home and think about what they had said, and I would close my door and cry tears like raindrops falling under an umbrella. So they made fun of me and said I was a parasol at a school of umbrellas, but I cried, "No, I'm an umbrella too, I just don't like the water. Why do we need to depend on water to be what we already are?" And I said, "Who are you to tell me how to be," and I tried to be strong and scary, and eventually I even bragged about how much I liked getting rained on, but they were never afraid of me, and they never believed me. And my parents always told me, "There's no umbrella sadder than the one that never gets opened in the rain." They said, "Someday, no matter how you feel, school's going to end." And I said, "Good!"

And they went on, "And when school ends the world's going to use you like the world uses umbrellas, because that's how they're going to see you." And I said to them, "What do I care?" But I said to myself, "Maybe I have to run away from this idiot world of umbrellas that live for the rain, and I have to escape all these people who are going to use me in ways that don't feel good to me." And I said, "Just because I *am* an umbrella doesn't mean I have to *be* an umbrella. Maybe I can be an umbrella in a completely different way." And I dreamt of giving a sleepy farmer shade at his fruit stand on the side of the highway. I dreamt of doing nothing at all in a dry room. Of writing my stories there. The martyr I think about most is Saint Sebastian because I have a friend named Sebastian. He's one of the few people I think would understand me because he writes stories too, and when you write stories you have to consider the way other people see the world. Nobody wants to read a story where every character has the same ideas. Sebastian writes stories. That's why he's nice to people who aren't like him. I've never told a human person how I feel about rain. Maybe I could tell Sebastian. It would be a hard conversation for me, but I think I can trust him, and I think he would understand. I see his face on Saint Sebastian's head every time I remember the story. I don't like seeing my friend Sebastian like that because I know what's coming, and it's not good. It always looks like a cartoon in my imagination. Like a photo of

Sebastian's face taped onto some medieval saint drawn by a monk who didn't actually know how to draw very well, but there was no one else around who even knew how to write, so he ended up with the feather and ink. I see it so clearly. Some angry people come along and tie my friend Sebastian to a tree. In my imagination I'm off to the side shouting, "Sebastian! Sebastian! Just pretend like you don't believe that stuff anymore! Tell them, 'No, of course, you're right, I'm sorry, I'm such a jerk,' and then go off and keep believing whatever you want somewhere they can't find you! Go to Venice! I heard that's a nice city. Or go up to the countryside around Amsterdam because the earth is golden there and the sunlight will make you think of God and you'll always feel like you're in good company!" But Saint Sebastian was stubborn. No matter how much he believed in Heaven, he must have felt scared. In my imagination I'm right there, but in the form of a lion, hiding off to the side in a bush, and I jump out to scare away the horrible people who've tied him up. But because it's a dream, or maybe because I'm visiting the past, it all happens like when Scrooge goes to visit Christmas Past and wants to interact with the world he's seeing, to change it and make it better, but he can't touch a thing, and nobody can see or hear him. I even try to slice away the ropes from around Sebastian's wrists and ankles, but my claws fade right through them, and he just goes on talking about his God, about how his God is the true one, the only one, "Hallelujah, Hallelujah," etc., and the people who tied him up shoot him with every arrow they have until they all think he's dead. And there's Sebastian, bleeding up there on a post, filled with arrows. It's the worst thing I could possibly imagine and, to make it worse, the scary people leave thinking they've won the battle. I wish Sebastian could have heard me when I said he should just lie. Then again, I guess people like Sebastian don't lie, so he wouldn't have listened to me anyways. Maybe he would have. Maybe the saints are terrible liars like everyone else. Some lies are pure evil. But lying isn't always so bad. I think if lying keeps you from getting killed so you can continue helping people in some way, then it's okay. Because then Sebastian could have continued living happily with that God of his, and who would have been hurt by that? Maybe he was a bad person. How should I know? I think his God is mean. I wonder if, when he first got hit by those arrows, he started to think that maybe God couldn't have possibly been real, or if he thought the whole thing was some valuable part of His plan all along. Anyways. There I am, standing there like a lion's ghost, or the ghost of some creature halfway between an umbrella and a lion, and a girl walks by and sees Sebastian tied to the tree, and she screams and rushes over to him. He's not quite dead. If I ever met her in real life I would give this girl a kiss because she was a friend to my friend Sebastian, but she died almost two thousand years ago. I don't think she even has a cheek to kiss anymore. She helped make him better. She must have loved him, and he must have loved her too. Love is like that. When the whole world, even you, thinks you're dead, it's the only thing that can bring you back to life. Because you have to want to be alive in order to come back to life, and that's what love makes you want. But instead of taking a hint and running off to Paris with this girl who came to save him, Sebastian had the bright idea of marching halfway-dead to the emperor's palace and declaring in the royal hall that he's still a Christian. God, Sebastian... So the emperor tells his henchmen to club Sebastian the other halfway to death. They do as they are told. And there goes Sebastian's body into the sewer. Can you imagine dying in a sewer and then still having people talk about you seventeen centuries later? I guess that's one kind of luck. I still wouldn't want to die like that. Too fancy. The truth is, I'm afraid to die at all. I'm just waiting for the rain to stop falling. Do you understand me, Sebastian? I wouldn't mind if the whole world turned into one big desert.

THE RADIO

A long rope hung from the back of the chair. It had been there for years. An old man came along, pushed it up one nostril, and pulled it out the other. When it came out, it was a snake, which wrapped itself around his neck and disturbed the old man's sense of wellbeing. A snake charmer, taking note of this transformation, began to play a tune. A dancer, taking interest in the music, began to oscillate his hips. The police, taking issue with the festivity, came and arrested the lot of these characters for disturbing the peace. The judge and jury were set up right there in the square. All were pardoned without ceremony, except the old man who had started it all by sticking the rope up his nose: he was sentenced to be hanged. Upon hearing the verdict of execution, the townspeople grew so impatient to enjoy the spectacle that they demanded the man be hanged right then and there with the rope already hanging from his nose, so they wouldn't have to wait a single minute longer.

And the old man with the rope in his nose was paraded to the gallows among shouts of glee. Meanwhile, the man and the snake had settled their differences and were at last on friendly terms. At this point the transmission cuts out, and I have to use my imagination to complete the story. I think about some possible endings: the snake pulling itself through the man's nose and saving him by squirting its venom onto the masses; the snake using the gallows' upper arm to lift the man up, Christlike, above the crowd, eclipsing the sun; the man's son witnessing his father's death, then walking away in tears, recollecting the happiness of his childhood, their summers on the island with Chester, the glaucoma-addled dog. I don't know. Who am I to say how

THE ESCALATOR MECHANIC

FOR PABLO KATCHADJIAN

"For weeks I haven't been able to focus on even the most trivial thing, because all I can think about is the shape of my right foot," the escalator technician confessed to me. He was clocking out of work. "Look at those escalators I was supposed to be servicing. They've all gone haywire, completely insane. Some of them slice the soles off their passengers' feet when they arrive at the landing. Some of them throw people straight off, like catapults. And others . . . others . . . don't even move at all . . ."

I didn't know what to tell my friend, except that perhaps, for the sake of everyone's safety, he should take some time off, go to the beach a week or two, relax, and let someone a little more competent—no, more composed—take his job for a while.

"But if I go to the beach, then I'll have to swim, which means I'll have to take off my shoes . . . and that will make everything worse. I don't want anyone else to see it…I don't even want to look at it myself."

To be honest, I was confused. Looking at his shoe I found no obvious peculiarities. So I asked him what about his foot had him so captivated, so afraid. He sighed, and told me not to worry. After all, he said, it wasn't my problem, and he didn't want to make it so, for fear that, once involved, I would, like him, never be able to extricate myself from what he referred to as his "curse of distraction."

A week later I was back at the mall, and everyone was in a huff because the escalators still weren't in working order. Those with wounded feet had left their few bloody footprints and collapsed. Bodies trebucheted from the escalators were strewn in heaps across the three floors of the mall. Impromptu medical camps had begun tending to the survivors. Shop owners on the upper levels were organizing in protest because they hadn't had any customers for weeks: the shoppers could only buy goods from the first floor, and besides, hardly anyone dared enter the mall anymore for the carnage. And people of all stripes, united in rare fashion, were blaming the escalator mechanic.

But this mechanic was no happy exception to the unhappy rule. Indeed, he may have been the most miserable of them all. And he took me aside, clearly in a desperate mood:

"I need someone else to know. I can't handle this alone anymore."

Out of sheer curiosity, I assented.

Upon my saying so, the man began to unlace his shoes, which, given the rawness of his grated soles, peeled off with great pain. Now, what he produced from underneath that leather Lovecraft himself would surely have described as ineffable, inarticulable, rapturously grotesque beyond language. But I'm not one to balk at a chance to dig into what others might find disgusting. In fact, I relish it. So, as much as my descriptions may inspire horrific images in your mind, please foreground, even before these images, the great pleasure I derive from relating them to you.

Out from the shoe first came the lower shin, which, transparent like a beer bottle, contained a brown, semi-boiling liquid that resembled—and smelled of—fermented apple cider. Through an opening in its side flew the hordes of fruit flies which, because of an inverted cone produced by the filth inside this cylinder, could not escape once they had entered. As a result, the ankle, which emerged next, was stuffed ever more densely with these insects, alive and dead, and I could not help but fear that its skin, which resembled a dun plastic shopping bag, would soon burst, releasing into the world some unseen and authentically dangerous illness. Out came the heel then, which at first glance seemed a miniaturized waterfall of incredible beauty, but soon revealed itself to be a poached ivory tusk of the recently extinct black rhinoceros, covered in a thick, steamy, oozing coat of Hollandaise sauce. The last thing to produce itself from that shoe was a broken web of muscles and veins, which dangled from the heel to the floor, and a head of hair wetted with spray adhesive: it swung freely, and yet remained bunched together by the congealing fluid it expelled. The flesh of his toes, he claimed, he had lost long ago in some other shoe, as well as their long bones, which once had traveled over the arch of his foot. The entire body part hung there at the end of his leg, pulsing like a heart, expanding and contracting like a lung, the rising and falling of Nature herself, and he looked between it and me through the spaces between his fingers, which covered his petrified face, anticipating the criticism he had feared so acutely those past few weeks.

I was speechless. My words prostrated in silence before my sense of awe.

"It's . . . a work of art," I whispered.

"I don't . . ." muttered the escalator mechanic. "It doesn't disgust you?"

"No, not at all . . . not one bit!"

"But . . ."

"Come to my house," I pleaded. "Please, come to my house. I need to photograph you."

"What? So everyone will know?"

"No, you fool!" I cried. "Because your foot makes me *feel* something. And I can't say the same about many things anymore. How jaded I've become! Ever since childhood,

I've been going along having these things we call *experiences* — each of which acts, at first, like a key to the next one that comes along and resembles it at all, and, later, like a blind that lies over it. That's to say, if I haven't already experienced something in itself, I've surely experienced something *like* it, and the similarity sits there like a lead blanket between the X-ray of my perception and whatever's going on around me. I'm numb...completely numb!...Am I making any sense?"

"Mmm...I can't tell."

"All I mean to say is that I've never seen anything like your foot before . . . and it's liberating, absolutely freeing, to see something entirely new."

"Well, it couldn't be *entirely* new. You just spent a page crafting ridiculous metaphors and similes comparing it to other things you've already seen. You'd have been more correct to, per Lovecraft, throw in the towel and call it indescribable, related to nothing, to no word, to . . ."

In the meantime, the crowd had grown emotional to a point of total incoherence, dragging the escalator mechanic into its bloodthirsty ranks, and the author of this story drunk to such an extent that he is unable to continue writing, viewing his effort — for the time being, anyhow — as a tedium and a failure.

THE GOOD IN HAVING
A NUCLEAR FAMILY

FOR JOSEF KAPLAN

Kit had such a pugnacious flu that he was forced to stay indoors all week. And all he could do was think about how he wanted to kill the President.

Lying in bed, feverish and unable to sleep for the sunlight pouring through his window, Kit believed he saw his mother Kate come into the room. "Mom," he said. "I've decided I want to kill the President. Nothing else I'm capable of in this life would have such a positive impact on the world."

"But first you'd have to kill the Vice President," she said, and Kit felt a pang of fear because he knew she was right.

Taking a hot shower to warm away his chills, Kit thought he heard someone enter the bathroom. He peeked his head out from behind the white curtain, and there stood his father, Fred, dressed like a doctor. "I heard you were sick, my child," he said.

"Three days now, and it hasn't gotten any better," said Kit, nodding. "You know, Dad, I've decided I have to kill the Vice President."

"What about the actual President?"

"Well, I want to kill him, too, but when I told Mom that, she pointed out that I'd have to kill the Vice President, to get to him."

"She's right, you know . . . and you know admitting that doesn't come easy," said Fred, as he turned into the towel on the floor. The towel continued speaking. "You might consider killing them both at the same time. Surer bet," it said. "But to get to them, you'll first have to take care of the Secretary of State, the Speaker of the House, the Attorney General. All those body guards . . . You know, the whole kit and kaboodle."

Splayed out on the couch beside a pot into which he had vomited, Kit was watching a movie. He remembered the story he once read about the king who died a thousand times—shot, quartered, tortured—and kept on reviving no matter how many times his subjects assassinated him. "I hope our President isn't so resilient," he said aloud.

"It's not only the President you need to worry about," his brothers Peter and Ben sang in chorus from the movie, dressed in shawls of fine silk.

"I know, I know. It just keeps getting more complicated . . ."

And so Kit went on, discussing these matters with increasingly remote family members, friends, and acquaintances, until he found himself discussing them with enemies and then even complete strangers, promising to wreak this death on political bodies further and further from the apparent source of his discontent, until Kit reasoned that, if he truly wanted to kill the President, he would first have to kill himself.

I AM NOT A HAPPY PERSON, AND I DON'T LIKE MY FRIENDS

A CARICATURAL ESSAY ON *THE 120 DAYS OF SODOM*

> *...if I saw your parched tongue hanging two feet out your mouth,*
> *I wouldn't offer you a single glass of water.*
>
> MARQUIS DE SADE

I am not a happy person, and I don't like my friends, so I go to the same café every day, where I know no one. It isn't a fancy café, but it is a sunny one on an otherwise fancy street. It's a café with families and elderly people and the occasional homeless man lingering at, or beside, its tables. The coffee is decent, though people tend to speak of it as if it were excellent.

It had been a long time since I'd ordered anything that day, and I was beginning to think the waitstaff wanted me gone, as they often do when I overstay my welcome, purchasing very little along the way but making sure to request glass after complementary glass of ice water. After all, I had the finest seat. The one on the patio. The one everyone fought over. The only seat that remained in the warm shade cast by the cathedral throughout the day, with no direct sunlight.

"Damn it to hell," I thought to myself when the man who, every day, offered to shine my black leather shoes—and who, upon my denial, would shake his head violently, as if in disbelief, scowling first at my shoes, then at my face— suddenly appeared, pointing from a distance at my feet. Admittedly, my shoes were a little scuffed, but such is my style. I don't think it hurts anyone.

Normally, he (I didn't know his name, nor he mine) controlled his aggression—a glance, a choice word, a stormy departure—but today, from the way he approached, I could tell his rage was less bridled, as if thoughts of me, of my unkempt shoes and, worse, my unwillingness to allow him to rejuvenate them, had occupied him over the course of a long, sleepless night. His evident fatigue seemed to be mingling with a spite made all the more acute by the fact that I was a foreigner here, a blue-eyed, goldilocked stranger, to boot, in the city he had always called home and had rarely left—and even then, only for some dreary reason: the funeral of a beloved grandparent, the upwardly-mobile wedding of a cousin whom he would have to watch be relieved of the shackles he knew would forever bind him to his class, of which I obviously knew very little, to this place I was merely flitting through—not disrespectfully, exactly, but inessentially, impermanently.

I must have truly been too rare a feast for his eyes that day because, after rushing me, in an attempt to take me by surprise, he seized my feet, grasping at my shoes, and began scrubbing them with a substance by the petrolic stink of which I realized was not shoeshine, but gasoline.

"This will be the last day I allow myself to look at your vile footwear! To whose faded leather I would prefer to see shopping bags full of vomit tied around your truncated ankles," he shrieked, binding my legs at the calf with a fearsome embrace.

No matter how I cried for help to the waitstaff—with some of whom I thought I'd established a quiet rapport—none of them came to my aid. Instead, they first watched on, and then, in fact, charged toward me as well, wielding belts and chains and tough rope, to lash me fast to my chair.

"Thank God we won't have to see those...*shoes* anymore," I heard Álvaro, my favorite barista, whisper to the shoeshiner.

"Don't thank God, you fool—thank *me*!" he hissed. And with burning eyes he set fire to my shoes, which went up like tinderboxes.

Thankfully, given my lengthy tenure on the café patio that day, I had consumed upwards of nine beverages, two of which were strong with caffeine and, thus, diuretic, plus seven complementary glasses of ice water, so my bladder was brimming with the fluid I realized could save me. The waitstaff had done a poor job of binding my arms, and without much effort I was able to liberate them. Unzipping my fly, I hastily released my member—altogether unremarkable in its flaccid state, but how could I let such questions of pride get in the way when, were I not to make use of this potentially underwhelming faucet now, I would have no member with which even to underwhelm, no body, perhaps not even a soul at all, in a matter of minutes—and I began to drain myself, making sure to give my tool the occasional jerk to splash the offender's head in piquant gestures of retaliation. But as soon as my urine touched his skin (the fire dutifully extinguished), he cried for me to continue, and once I was fully emptied, demanded that I be bound again and transported to the back room of the café. So the waitstaff carried me like a queen of old in her litter, or a Jew on his wedding day, to a part of the café I had never seen before, which we accessed through a false door behind the toilet in the men's room.

What must the other patrons have thought, having beheld that spectacle, then witnessing me, with smoke still rising from the tips of my legs, be carried by this raging crowd of at least six into, though not back out of, a bathroom fit for a maximum of one, as clowns into the clown car?

The hidden chamber was tall and tiled with an array of small mirrors, its ceiling gracefully vaulted and adorned with frescoes of cherubs bearing floral sprigs up to otters, squirrels, and other sylvan beasts. Not that I had much of a chance to appreciate its finery; for, placing me, bound once more, at the center of the room on a crudely hewn marble pedestal, the shoeshiner demanded that I be forced to drink another gallon of water and, for diuretic purposes, funnel-fed at least four more espressos. The sum would have been greater, I heard him explain, had he not already witnessed me consume more than enough to materially accelerate my need to micturate. And so, they saw to it that I drink like a hose in reverse.

"What you did out there—" the shoeshiner began.

"I was so shocked," I interrupted, "that I couldn't help but get a bit on you... I'm s—"

"No, my child!" he cut back in. "I only hope there's more where that came from!"

Aside from Álvaro, the entire waitstaff, seeing that its work was done—and perhaps also preferring not to witness what was soon to transpire—shuffled back out of the room through the bathroom's trap door. Oddly enough, it was only Gabriela, a server with whom I had only rarely inter-acted, who showed any hint of sympathy, shooting me a brief but merciful glance and blowing me a clandestine kiss on her way out, as if to say good-bye, fare thee well, until the next world.

"Now," said Álvaro, "let it be known that this man does not want to take you as his companion. Nor does he wish to see your face, hear your voice, know anything about your personal life, or establish any other thread of potential intimacy with you." And with this, he placed an opaque black bag over my head.

"Why have you brought me here?" Words which could hardly escape my mouth.

"For two reasons," Álvaro answered. "First—"

"To shine those little Oxfords of yours," said the shoeshiner.

"And second—" said Álvaro.

"That you might bathe me in your urine!" the shoeshiner howled.

I'd heard of people like these. But until that point I'd taken them to be the figments of some sick old author's imagination.

For half an hour, the shoeshiner applied himself to vigorously cleansing my shoes of the gasoline and urine which had penetrated their upper. All the while, Álvaro accompanied this delirious frottage with melodies on a cello, facing a corner decked with mirrors. I couldn't quite put my finger on what it was he was playing—figuring this out, as you might imagine, was not high on my list of priorities—but I remember it as having been baroque, unceasing in its minor arpeggiation, reminiscent of certain moodier passages from Bach's second Cello Suite.

Once my shoes were sufficiently clean, the shoeshiner dropped to his knees before me and laced them back onto my feet. He cried out to Álvaro, who by now I was certain

115

had no dissimulated plan to rescue me, and told him to hold my head angled downward toward my shoes. Wedging his thumbs painfully behind my ears and digging his fingers into my temples and cheeks, Álvaro obeyed without question.

"Álvaro, please!" I shouted so loudly my throat burned dry, half hoping to catch a shred of empathy large enough to tear him out of whatever spell he had apparently fallen under, half hoping some patron (if indeed any remained) might overhear and alert the authorities. Neither hope bore fruit. Instead, my effort, in its failure, served only to confirm the inevitability of my proximate suffering.

From his crouched position on the floor, the shoeshiner gazed up at my face with a smile easily recognizable as insane—possessed, even—channeling lubricious evils of which he had never more than dreamt, as if he were unexpectedly departing our world, the rules of which he had only begrudgingly claimed to accept, for a paradise of boundless possibility where he alone reigned king.

My member, which still rested on the drenched cotton around my open fly, and the clenched urethra connecting it to my overfull bladder, were the only things separating him from the newly processed fluids inside me. And as he began shining my shoes, his smile growing ever more menacing, he shouted, from foot of the pedestal, "Release it, why don't you! You rake! Let your golden liqueur flow upon me!"

"Do as he says, man!" snapped Álvaro, in whose tone I sensed an urgency, as if he were begging me to follow the shoeshiner's instructions, perhaps for my own good.

Knowing this possibility as my last hope, I let my "golden liqueur" flow upon him. I'd drunk such a quantity that the stream was immense, and so much was passing through me that I feared my urethra might tear, when, moments later, I felt a stinging pain and my product turned from a pale, almost undetectable, yellow, to a rusty umber that signaled my fear had come true.

The urine soared in its Newtonian arc through the air before me and splashed over the shoeshiner's head, parting his hair as he shagged his mane back and forth, his eyes tightly—ecstatically—shut. With one hand he held my right shoe, and with the other he shined it, roaring with a lubricity and pleasure of which I, in turn, had never so much as dreamt—such that, for an instant, I even felt the intimations of a jealous emotion.

While the shoeshiner, blinded by his pleasure, received my gift by gravity's grace, I felt Álvaro's hands release my head. And shooting my gaze suddenly to the side, I witnessed him pick up from the floor a great car battery hooked up to live, lashing wires—how he smuggled this in, I will never know—and, chopping his flat left hand into the course of my stream, so as to disconnect my body from the pooling liquid it was ejecting, he used his right hand to hurl this battery and its exposed cables at the sopping shoeshiner. And upon contact, the man who had so recently been the world's most unspeakably happy individual transformed into a lifeless mound of smoky, twitching flesh.

"Álvaro!" I cried. "I knew you wouldn't just watch it happen!"

The scent in the room was foul—although, as Álvaro began to speak, removing the bag from my head, a certain carnal note in the rising smoke struck me, I admit, as appetizing.

"Where shall we begin, Kit *Schluter*?"

I looked at him in awe.

"How do you know my last name?"

"Let's just say I'm attentive to certain customers' receipts."

"Please, just let me go," I pleaded.

"Oh, this is only the beginning . . . For, you see, Kit, I believe in procreation. I believe in God, the family, the value of structures that bind us to repetition," Álvaro declared. "From what I have observed, you most certainly do not share these beliefs."

"I said, let me out of here!" I shouted, thrashing against the ropes binding me to my chair.

"Look at you," Álvaro scoffed, "big adventurer in a foreign country. You moved here because you knew no one.

You sit there writing a book you'll never finish writing while reading five others you'll never finish reading. You rarely shower. You don't have a steady job. You have zero marketable skills. You're confused about your sexuality, yet you barge ahead with your haphazard games of seduction, and you disdain yourself for it. You fear marriage, any form of commitment. With the first hint of dissatisfaction comes the flood of alienation. You're cagey, but worse—because you've always suspected this is what makes you attractive, for isn't it exactly what draws *you* in?—you're flighty. Perfectly here one day, perfectly gone the next, off on some fresh quest for Novelty. How can anyone trust you, you ask, how can anyone be trusted? In your eyes, learning trust is a fool's errand. You reserve your desires for unattain—"

"If you're going to lecture me, you could at least be a little more charitable," I snapped, hoping to put an end to his senseless derision.

Ever since he started talking, the smell around us had lost its appetizing note and become simply nauseating.

"You'll tell me that we've hardly ever spoken, won't you, Kit? Nothing more than banter while you order, a little chit-chat over the check?"

"And wouldn't that be fair?"

"Oh, but I see you every day. Out there, vying for that seat on the patio. The one everyone fights over. And I watch you talk—to very few people, perhaps, but still, I watch you talk. I hear your words when you're accompanied; I watch where your eyes fall when you're alone—on what, on whom . . . Oh, where eyes fall says so much! You're so arrogant you probably think I have no idea about any of those books you read, but I've recognized my share. And let me tell you: they are terrible, terrible works."

"Terrible?"

"Against God! Against the family! Against Nature! *Damn* you!"

"Name one decent book that promotes family values."

"Let's say . . . *A Farewell to Arms*. I overheard you chatting about it just last week with that . . . that *vagrant* you invite to your table."

"*A Farewell to Arms*? Family values?"

"Yes, the love story to end all love stories! For its love leads to a child!"

"I've always understood that book as Hemingway murdering his own domestic instinct."

"What's that, now?"

"If you think about it, there's no child at all, no family. Just the mirage of a desire for such things. Catherine—the nurse he falls in love with, remember?—she dies on the last page giving birth to a stillborn fetus."

"Oh, I recall . . . but tell me more," Álvaro demanded.

"If either Catherine or the child had lived, I don't think Hemingway would have found the adventure worth writing about. No unforgettable sex in the hospital bed, no canoeing across Lake Como in the dead of night with bleeding palms. And believe me, the end destroys me every time—it's one of the few books to have ever made me cry, and even on repeat readings. But recently, the more I've thought about it, the more I've felt tricked by all that mourning. You can tell, he even has fun writing the death scene—the way he compares the lifeless fetus to a dead rabbit...True sorrow gives way far short of such clever imagery. That's what first led me to believe that there's a sick indulgence underlying it all. Their deaths unburden him of his future with them, and that's what allows him to wax so sentimental about their relationship without risk."

"Risk of...?"

"Of making a promise he'd have to make good on. Of committing to a lifelong marriage with Catherine, to decades of raising that child. His relief that they're not around anymore is precisely what allows him to feel so crushed, yet so free to dream. Don't you see? It's all so cynical, a masquerade of grief. Within the book, Henry, Hemingway's avatar, is so sensitive, so in love, but seen from without, as the person out there in the physical world typing up the story, Hemingway's just another man who's terrified of commitment — to such an extent that he can't even bear to live it out in a book."

"Sounds a bit like you, doesn't he?"

"I'm not planning on shooting myself in the head any time soon."

"How would you feel if the love of your life got pregnant with your child?"

"What's it to you if I want a child or not?"

"My question concerns human nature."

"Human nature?"

"The shoeshiner didn't want kids either. That's why, in the end, I didn't hesitate to stop him."

"You've stopped making sense."

"Look, Kit. That man wanted to submit you absolutely to his will, to play God with you — but for what? To quench his personal thirsts. But what good is pleasure if it ends in pleasure? You see, for the shoeshiner, it took total control, total submission, to feel even the first rumbling of satisfaction. He once told me that the only ideal he served was novelty, the enemy of which he saw as repetition, which, in turn, he viewed as fundamental to any and all of my own value syst—"

"Why didn't you help me sooner?"

"I had accepted his bribe. We all had. Ultimately, though, I couldn't stand by and watch his pleasure being channeled hedonistically inward, rather than exercised in the service of procreation."

"You knew about this before?" I snapped.

Álvaro nodded with a hint of shame.

"If he'd been doing it all to facilitate the birth of a child," he said, "I swear I would have let it go on. Why are we here in the first place? For the sake of the race—to have children."

"You talk a big game. Do you have any yourself?" I asked.

"Three beautiful daughters. Here," said Álvaro, taking out his phone, "I'll show you a pict—"

"Put that away! You're out of your mind."

"How dare you?"

"Listen, Álvaro," I said after a pregnant silence. "Maybe you're onto something, after all. Are you ready to hear what I really think?"

"I am!" cried Álvaro, his face filled with hope.

"Your ideas are bullshit. Your take on me is bullshit. This café is bullshit. The people who just watched on and did nothing, the whole staff that let this happen for some pocket change, this secret room—bullshit—bullshit—bullshit. And you know what? I'm starting to think that *I'm* bullshit, too. Funny thing is, the only one who doesn't seem like bullshit to me right now is the shoeshiner."

Álvaro looked hurt. He told me that he only wanted to keep talking, but I'd made up my mind. It was time to leave this piss-soaked café and never return. I shouted belligerently until he untied me, then I walked across the room, stepping over the shoeshiner's smoking, redolent corpse, turned the handle to the false door, and crept my way into the bathroom behind the toilet. A man relieving himself in my direction squealed with shock. In his surprise, he jerked, and his stream ricocheted off the top of the toilet, splashing onto my chin. So I sighed and returned to the back room, waiting for him to finish, my ear pressed to the trap door. And when I heard the toilet flush, it was then that I fled this café and hid behind the locked door of my rented room until I knew the coast was clear—

But the coast was never clear.

GIUSEPPE CESARI, PORTRAITIST

The soporific effects of the long vowels I had been cooing along my early evening walk had strengthened, especially that of the O, which I once dreamt sat atop Giuseppe Cesari's head like a wreath. And without a thing to do this eleventh of March, and with no distracting company in my apartment aside from the feral cats who passed through whenever they pleased to eat from the dishes of curdled milk I left out for them, I went not home for a nap but instead to pay this esteemed, though per my opinion mediocre, painter Cesari a visit, with the intention of commissioning one of his younger, less expensive, but potentially more talented, acolytes to paint my mother's deathbed portrait.

I was greeted at the front door without suspicion by his two sons, Muzio and Bernardino, who, upon my telling them of my intentions, directed me where I might go in order to negotiate the matter with their father. Before sending me on my way, however, they warned me of the likelihood of my outright dismissal. For without exception, they said nearly in unison, he was surly and dyspeptic in his interactions with strangers. It struck me as curious that they chose not to accompany me, a stranger, through the hallways of their own father's treasure-laden estate, when suddenly I heard, rattling down the marble halls, a tittering of young women ring out from the very garden back to which they had rushed after letting me in. The early spring air in the long hallways was stagnant and damp, as if this night were the first time since autumn that their windows had been thrown open. Outside, the night air was crisp, and from upstairs the visibility over the bric-a-brac rooftops of the city was clear and far-reaching.

Cesari's salon, situated at the end of a long gallery containing several generations of family portraiture, was bathed in the inoffensive glow of candlelight. So filled, in fact, was the room with candles, and so various their placement, that no object cast any shadow at all. When I entered — my pant legs rolled up to just below my knees, I recall, having come directly from my walk through the Campo de' Fiori — I did not introduce myself, but remarked straightaway on the rich smell of what I imagined to be rosemaried meats and roasted sugars that wafted through the room, mixing along the way with the scent of fresh minced fruit and fermented grape.

"Certain things allow themselves to happen," Cesari said as both greeting and reply, "while others do not, being afraid of the judgment to which all things imaginable are subject."

I asked him what relation he found between his observation and my comment, to which he replied there was none; I had simply interrupted his thought, he said, and he had wanted to give voice to it before his memory "pissed it away." And so I gave him a moment to reflect, looking out at the constellation of open windows glowing on the Collis Quirinalis.

"Do you know the color of the carnation while it is still in the bud?" he asked.

I waited, with back still turned, for his response to the rhetorical question.

"Well—?" he insisted. I remained silent. "Let me tell you, then. As the blood in our bodies, so a carnation in its bud, is a bright shade of blue. Yet this color changes abruptly upon the petals' exposure to the air. Sealed inside, the petals have not yet enjoyed the good fortune of breathing the fresh air of this Earth, but when the bud opens at last, even the slightest bit, the veins running along petals' surface rupture, and their contents—the flower's very blood, you might say—spill out."

I turned to face him. He was looking down the hallway, speaking slowly, as if to someone who had already left.

"Therefore it could be said that the color of the petal is the result of a wound. It's as when one submerges his wrist in olive oil, which, as we know, contains no oxygen, and slits it: the blood that clouds out into the oil is blue, and the loss of this blue—not crimson—liquid is what quickly leaves him dead. How queer to think the loss of something so familiar, in such an unrecognizable form, could carry away his very life..."

LIKE A CLOUD CAN DO

My dad says that when he was a little girl like me he had a thousand cactuses. There were yellow ones and purple ones and cactuses of many colors that looked like cars and trees. But his favorite cactus of all acted like a cloud. Every time he looked at it and looked away and then looked back again it changed shape. Remember that clouds can take the shape of everything in the world, so sometimes it looked like nothing at all (like a cloud can do) but sometimes it looked like a monk or even a coffee pot (like a cloud can do, too). Sometimes, he says, it even looked like his other cactus which looked like a baby tiger.

One day my dad's parents lost their jobs because of a war that had ruined their city and they had to move to another country that doesn't exist anymore. They walked and rode in strangers' wagons and even snuck onto freight trains, and my dad promised me that they were happy even though they were hungry and had lots of dandruff in their hair and dirt under their fingernails.

Well, the only thing my dad kept from his old bedroom was his favorite cactus. When they got to the biggest city in that country that doesn't exist anymore, my dad brought his cactus to a famous market where there was a renowned expert in rare plants who also happened to know a great deal about religious things. The man was fat and wore all of his clothes backwards because that way no one could tell what he was thinking.

By this time, my dad was thirteen and his family was so poor that they lived in a single bedroom with five other families and two dogs and more than five cats. So he decided that, however much he loved his cactus, he should sell it in order to buy a small house for them.

Not long after, my dad went to the market to show his cactus to the fat plant man who wore all his clothes on backwards and ask how much he would buy it for. The plant man took out his magnifying glass and brought the plant close to his face. For the first time ever the cactus did not keep changing shapes, but remained in a single one. It looked just like the Buddha's tooth.

The expert knew he could make a great deal of money off such a tooth and thought to himself, "What a fool this foreign girl must be . . . She thinks the Buddha's tooth is a cactus!" And even though he thought my dad couldn't read his wicked mind because his clothes were on backwards, my dad saw right through him.

First, the man offered five hundred rubles for the plant, but my dad was smart and said no. Then he offered ten thousand rubles. But my dad said he would only take fifty thousand rubles for the cactus because it was his favorite. The man thought for a moment and decided that it was still a good deal for him, so he handed my dad a sack of fifty thousand rubles right then and there and considered himself the cleverest man on Earth.

But as soon as my dad was out of sight the cactus started changing into horrible things. First, it changed into a dead elephant's eyeball crawling with insects and bugs, and the man pounded his table because he knew he had been tricked. Then it took the shape of a rhinoceros tusk stuck into the plant man's very own left eye socket, and the man became afraid of the cactus and hid it under his table. The next day my dad returned to the market and stole his cactus back when the man wasn't looking, and when he got home the cactus turned into the shape of a cloud that looked like nothing at all.

That's why I have my dad's cactus with me here now, and as I watch it change shapes it is telling me this story.

THE STRUCTURE OF OUR ARGUMENTS

If you only knew how I would like to bite into your heart
and drink your life very very slowly, without raising my head.

MARGUERITE BURNAT-PROVINS

Morning dawns. The curtains are shut. In the dark, the mother awakes from a dream and rubs her eyes. She looks at the ceiling while her mind comes to life.

"I am no longer dreaming," she thinks.

"I am no longer dreaming," she says aloud.

She stands up from the bed and draws the curtains. In the sunlight, she puts on a robe.

"I am no longer dreaming."

In the kitchen, she lights a match and ignites the stove under the coffee press. She watches it absent-mindedly until the coffee percolates. She pours herself a cup and allows the fragrant steam to waft up to her nose.

In the living room, the baby is asleep in a crib. The mother walks over to the baby and gazes upon his sleeping face. She kisses him on the forehead. The baby awakes, and looks at his mother with the very gaze a baby gives his mother when she is the first thing he sees upon waking.

"Ba boo boo ba ba," he babbles.

"You are no longer dreaming," she says.

"I love you," she says.

The baby drools and laughs. She takes him in her arms and, together, they waltz around the living room. Softly, she sings him a song.

"Those green eyes..." she croons. "So serene, so wise..."

When the mother stops singing, the baby kicks her in the chest with his bare foot.

"Ba boo ba boo boo," he says.

The mother laughs. "So, you want me to keep singing?" she asks.

"Boo boo, ba *beh*!" he says, and kicks her again, though much harder this time—somehow, she could swear, with the strength of an adolescent.

The mother holds the baby out in front of her as his legs thrash back and forth, trying to kick her once more.

"So that's how it's going to be, is it?" the mother asks, and puts the baby on the floor.

She pulls back her leg, and decides to kick the baby with all her might. At the very last moment, however, she stops her foot beside his chest and tickles him in the armpit with her toes. The baby laughs.

"Bee bee bo ba ba," he says.

"What's that, baby?" she asks.

"Bee bee bo *ba* ba!" he says, and begins to cry.

"You want me to kick you for real this time?" she asks.

"Ba *ba!*" he says, smiling placidly.

Once again, the mother reels back her leg, hesitates, and then commits. This time her kick lands square in the baby's ribs, and his diminutive body goes tumbling across the room. When it stops, it lies, motionless and face down, on the floor.

The mother looks at the baby, realizing with horror what she has done. She walks slowly across the room, her fingers trembling before her lips.

"Baby?" she says. "Baby, can you hear me?"

The baby says nothing. He appears not to be breathing.

"Oh, god . . . ," says the mother.

She kneels down beside the baby, and rolls him over so that his face is facing hers. The head, slack on his neck; the eyes closed; the chest as still as a rock.

"Baby . . . Baby, please," she says, and leans her head down to listen to his heartbeat. "Baby, breathe for me . . . Please wake up . . . I didn't mean to . . ."

Just then, the baby opens his eyes and throws his hands out theatrically to his sides, shouting, "Boo baa, *boo boo ba baa!*"

And he kicks his mother square in the nose—somehow, she could swear, with the strength of a full-grown adult.

PARABLE OF THE VERY NARRATIVE STRUCTURE AT PLAY IN THIS PARABLE

Because all narratives are endless, that makes
the initiating of narratives far more important
than the resolution of narratives.

DALLAS WIEBE

After completing a draft of a children's book called *The Hatter's Tripod Wife*, the Maid Who Was Secretly a Children's Book Author fell into a flower bed, then she fell into a bottle of bleach. When she crawled back out of the bottleneck, her hair was white, and her skin even whiter. So the Master's Cat mistook her for a great, human-sized mouse, and she licked her lips with appetite well whetted and stomach all a-grumble.

"Oh, little Kitty!" cried the Maid Who Was Secretly a Children's Book Author. "I simply must tell you. I've just finished writing my first book, and I couldn't be happier with how it turned out. Listen closely, because it all gets moving fast. It tells the story of a rich woman with three legs and her husband, a poor hat-maker who spends his entire inheritance on a pair of three-legged pants for her."

"Incredible...," murmured the Master's Cat. "I've never met such a large mouse before, let alone one who writes children's books." Then she fantasized of how tender and sweet such a large, intellectual brain must taste, and her mouth grew wet with the saliva that shot out in lustrous streams from under her tongue.

"Well, one day this poor hatter visits a tailor who specializes in odd-limbed luxury clothing. But when the tailor states the price of the pants, our man quickly sees that a single pair will cost his entire nest egg—a modest sum he has only just inherited after the death of his parents, which I leave unexplained, for the sake of mystery, you see. But the hat-maker loves his wife so much, and believes, like many men, that the husband's duty is to lavish his wife with impractically expensive gifts, that he goes right ahead and buys the three-legged pants for her. And so he finds himself impoverished."

By now, the Master's Cat was getting quite hungry. And alongside her hunger grew her impatience to sink her fangs into the Maid's delectable brain. "Look," began the Master's Cat, knowing it impolite to eat someone who was in the middle of a story, but hoping to expedite the arrival of its conclusion, so she might get on with her meal. "You should know this about me: I don't care much for beginnings—nor, mind you, for middles. I don't even care for climaxes...

I'm neutered, anyhow! What I love most about a story is its resolution . . . a nice, clean, fast ending."

"Oh, Kitty," said the Maid. "This might be a problem . . . You see, I don't believe in endings, so my children's book certainly won't offer what you're looking for. A novelist I enjoy once said, 'Resolution isn't important because no narrative is ever resolved or can be resolved.' Why battle the obvious?"

And the Master's Cat, too hungry to wait any longer for the fledgling author to finish her narration, sauntered off to the kitchen to eat the cut of fish her master had left out for her that morning. And while she ate her salmon, along with half a stale loaf of bread, she composed the beginning of a poem in her mind, which went like this:

> *Fire licked at the barrel of oats*
> *while the children made bread out of dust.*
> *I'll sing of these babies till their eyes turn blue*
> *and all my body's fruit floats off to heaven . . .*

DOG PERSON

Today I sat in the shallow sea trying to pet the foam of the waves, as if it were a dog.

The foam approached, I reached out, and it ran away every time with such determination that it disappeared, as if it were a cat.

For this I loved the foam, and I reached toward it with ever greater obstination.

PRIDE

People often say they stopped reading a book as a way of criticizing it: "I started it, but I put it down."

"I put even books I like down," I say, in direct criticism of myself.

"But the books I love most I'd never dare finish," I think, in oblique praise of myself.

Fin

ACKNOWLEDGMENTS

A number of these cartoons appeared—some in slightly different form—in the magazines *The Baffler, Black Sun Lit, The Brooklyn Rail, Castle Grayskull,* and *New York Tyrant;* the chapbooks *5 Cartoons/5 caricaturas* (Juan Malasuerte Editores, 2019; tr. Mariana Rodríguez) and *The Good in Having a Nuclear Family* (Despite Editions, 2019); and the anthology *Best American Experimental Writing 2020* (Wesleyan UP, 2020). Many thanks to all of the editors and collaborators who made these publications possible; many thanks now, as well, to the entire crew at City Lights for this incarnation.

As for the epigraphs, there were a few instances where existing translations were too *perfect* to resist including. The Marguerite Burnat-Provins epigraph was translated by Cassia Berman from *Le Livre pour toi [The Book for You]* and encountered in *A Book of Women Poets from Antiquity to Now* (Schocken, 1992); the André Gide epigraph was translated by Dorothy Bussy from *Les Nourritures terrestres* (*The Fruits of the Earth,* Secker & Warburg, 1949); and the Marquis de Sade epigraph was translated by Will McMorran and Thomas Wynn, from *Les 120 journées de Sodome* (*The 120 Days of Sodom*, Penguin Classics, 2016). The remaining epigraphs are presented in my translation.

I send gratitude to the many friends and family members who have spurred my imagination by talking over and offering their thoughts on these stories, and by simply sharing their company with me, all of which has played its part in coaxing these writings into their current shapes. Credit goes to Alex Moll for the punchline at the end of "Example of a Plotline," and particularly emphatic nods are due to Garrett Caples, editor of this book, as well as my brothers, Peter and Ben, who taught me to love cartoons.

Now, it's your turn: